I0619498

NOW
YOU
DON'T

Now You Don't

book 3 of the Eldritch Novels series

Copyright © 2018 by Tom Leveen

Cover design:
FTJ Creative LLC

All rights reserved. No part of this book may be reproduced in any form by any electronic or mechanical means including photocopying, recording, or information storage and retrieval without permission in writing from the author.

This is a work of fiction. Names, characters, businesses, places, events and incidents are either the products of the author's imagination or used in a fictitious manner. Any resemblance to actual persons, living or dead, or actual events is purely coincidental.

ISBN: 978-1-952582-06-6

Printed in U.S.A

NOW

YOU

DON'T

TOM LEVEEN

●II
FTJ Creative LLC

Scottsdale, Arizona

Enjoy these books by Tom Leveen:

Party

Zero

manicpixiedreamgirl

Sick

Random

Shackled

Violent Ends (anthology)

Hellworld

Mercy Rule

A Little Insurrection Now & Then

Those We Bury Back

Heartless

For aspiring writers:

How To Write Awesome Dialogue!

How To Write Your Novel by Watching Movies First

NOW
YOU
DON'T

Tom Leveen

ONE

Travis awoke believing he was having a heart attack but instead it was a monster. It perched on his chest, weighing him down, pressing him into his memory foam mattress until it took the shape of an Egyptian sarcophagus. The thing must have weighed more than a hundred pounds; two hundred, maybe. It had knees, for they were pressed into the hollows of Travis's shoulders, preventing him from moving his arms. He thought its feet were positioned in such a way as to keep his thighs immobile as well. The thing apparently knew Brazilian jiu-jitsu because holy shit he could not move.

He had only enough time upon waking to see that it had a tiny hole of a mouth, a small black disc in the darkness of his bedroom that reminded him absurdly of a blow-up doll, though he'd never actually seen one of those in person. The skin of its cheeks was pulled taut, giving the thing a gaunt, ghoulish appearance. Its skin was something on the Caucasian spectrum, not quite pale and not quite tan. The forehead rose high and sloped backward with sparse baby hair sprouting along the crown. The fineness of the hair reminded Travis of his daughter's scalp when she'd been born twelve years ago.

Darla, he thought as the terror of his situation lit his nerves on fire. Darla, where is she?

The monster was naked. In the half-second Travis's brain had to assess all these facts, it also registered that some small, limp, cold limb lay across his belly. A penis, chilled and damp, as if having emerged from a swimming pool.

"Whut—" A sound less than a word belched from Travis's mouth as the thing atop him tilted its head, staring down with blue eyes lit by the beam of a streetlight shooting from between the dark wood blinds.

The monster raised its right hand. It looked spider-like in the dark, shadowy and segmented. Its nails were overgrown, inches long, jagged and sharp.

It tilted its head again before plunging a finger into the soft skin where Travis's eyelid met his eye socket.

Travis had enough air to scream as the finger pierced deep. The monster drove its finger down, then to the right. Travis felt the rough skin and sharp claw sliding behind his eyeball and heard the chilling squish of the eye popping neatly, though not cleanly, from out of his skull.

The monster laid its other hand across Travis's mouth as he bellowed. The skin of its palm was calloused, warm, and dry. Every muscle in his body cramped as Travis fought against the monster's weight, against the fear for Darla's little life, against the rich, bright pain in the cavern where his eye used to be.

He felt a tug deep in his skull, like tightening a shoelace. Then a brisk snap and the eye let go from its mooring.

Travis's other eye, his right, was wide open. Even in

the dark and despite the rampage of cascading hormones released by pain and terror, Travis's one remaining eye beheld the monster as it held up its hand. The eye swung from the monster's finger tip by the stalk, wide by default since it had no lids, gazing blindly back at its owner, accusing. Travis wanted to vomit, wanted to pass out, wanted the horror to end.

Darla! he screamed, but the sound was incoherent and muffled under the creature's palm. Travis tried to close his eye but couldn't—a warm disbelief flooded his system, convincing him this was a dream, what else could it be, surely this was a nightmare from which he would awake any second now, *any second now* . . .

The monster tilted its head back and raised its hand, dangling the eyeball above its face. It issued a short sucking sound. Travis heard it, or imagined he heard it, over his ongoing muffled screams. The eye slipped neatly into the beast's circular mouth.

It lowered its chin to stare at Travis as its jaw worked. It studied him as a bird might study a worm. Travis stopped screaming, overcome with wretched disgust and nausea as he watched the monster eat. The thing itself didn't seem to blink, or if it did, it was too quick for Travis to notice.

Of course, what he really noticed was that he had just had his left eye pulled out and eaten by a naked humanoid monster.

Perhaps, Travis considered mildly in that cobwebbed corner where such space is reserved for insane thought, that is what I should be focused on right now.

His cries for Darla shifted to a cry for help. The monster gave him what was, for all intents and purposes, a pitying look. It then curled its right hand over his left eye and began working at it as he had the other.

Right-handed, Travis's brain pointed out. Look at that, it's right-handed and having a little trouble. That must be why this one hurts more. Oh, wait—*Look* at that? Haha, I get it. Very punny.

His voice went coarse as he lost all vision. The dark world in front of him did not fade to black or red or white; it simply ceased to see in one quick pop. The eye came out less gracefully than the left had. Explosive pressure burst somewhere just above his face, and Travis felt the viscous goo of the eyeball drip onto his cheek. Then came a slurping noise and his brain advised he not think about what that sound meant.

Please, he begged silently through his raw screams. Please don't let me die please not like this sweet Jesus God please don't let this be how I go out please . . .

The weight vanished. Travis bolted upright, hands flying to his face, covering his cavernous eye sockets. The space left behind sickened him and his pizza dinner burst forth from his mouth, coating his boxers and naked thighs, still warm from where the creature had perched.

Senselessly he swung his hands down for a pillow, which he found and stuffed against his face. His brain, operating on brute instinct, questioned whether or not bleeding to death were a real possibility.

Someone would come now, he thought, or semi-thought; conscious words were well beyond his abilities now. Someone would hear what passed for screams and come running, call the cops, call the paramedics, they'd get here, save his life . . .

But because of the depth and breadth of his screams, his voice was utterly destroyed. All that came out were slick tendrils of puke and a hoarse grunting that no one could hear past his own bedroom door.

Instinctively he got to his knees on the mattress, swiping his bookshelf headboard for his cell phone. He found it readily in its usual place beside his framed photo of Jenny and Darla and got it into his hands where it rested with its knobby, familiar comfort.

He groaned, then wailed as the futility of it hit him—if it was a landline and he could calm down enough to rationalize, he could have called 911 by feeling for the buttons. But a touch screen? The chances of guessing what numbers he was hitting, if any at all, were remote at best. He remembered there was some push-button way to automatically dial the emergency number, but could *not* remember what the hell it was.

"Fuck!" Travis screeched noiselessly, the first actual word he'd managed to form since the monster had climbed onto him.

The monster—where?

Panicked, Travis slid from the bed and huddled against the wall, drawing his knees up to his chest and scrambling for the pillow again to staunch the blood and gore he felt trailing warmly down his face. Where had it gone? Still in the room? He bit the pillow to force himself into silence and listened.

No sound but his own pumping heart and the short snorts of breath from his nose against the pillowcase. The floor was carpeted, it could be standing right in front of him for all he knew.

Travis kicked out. His feet scraped carpet, but nothing else.

Darla—

He heard no screams from her room. Maybe the thing didn't know about her or didn't care. Or maybe it had already silently killed her in her sleep before coming for him.

Or, or, or . . .

Groaning again Travis tossed the pillow aside and crawled forward. He'd be lined up with his bedroom door from here. Whether or not the thing that had blinded him was still here or not, he couldn't help that. He could think of no practical way to defend himself against it if it attacked again. That left Darla, making sure she was safe somehow.

But if he couldn't defend himself, how could he possibly—

Travis let the thought fly away. No helping that now. He had to know if his daughter was safe.

He found his bedroom door open. Maybe that meant it had left; he slept with the door closed, he and Jenny always had back when they actually shared a house. He crept past the threshold and turned right, knees abrading from carpet burns.

"Darla!" he croaked, reaching out with his left hand, sweeping broadly, seeking the dip in the wall that would indicate her doorframe. His fingers found the lip and he pulled himself toward it, calling her name again.

Darla's door was shut. He shoved stupidly, blindly into it for a moment before reaching up for the door knob and twisting with one slick hand.

Travis fell into the door which flew open and banged against the wall.

"Darla!"

He heard her mumble something nonsensical, then say, "Dad?" A catch in her voice gave it two syllables.

Travis rose to his knees and said her name, reaching out for her.

A moment of silence followed, broken next by his daughter's piercing, endless scream.

○

Jim didn't know whether to knock or just what, so he let himself into the hospital room without announcing himself. He later berated himself for the truth: he wanted to see what he'd be getting into first. He wanted to get half a look at Travis before committing to going into the room, because Jesus Christ, what if he was all gored up and shit? Unlikely, given their location, but still. The image and idea stuck in his head.

He peeked around the wall and saw Travis in a room by himself, his head and eyes bandaged thickly with bright white gauze. No blood stained the wraps. He lay quiet and still, mouth slightly ajar, breathing on his own with a slow, regular rhythm. Some invisible man was talking to Travis, and it took Jim another second to realize it was an audiobook whispering from Travis's phone, which lay on a nearby tray beside a yellow plastic pitcher.

"Am I awake? Who's there?"

Travis's voice was dry and ragged, but his face—the half Jim could see of it—didn't tense.

"Hey, man," Jim said, sliding closer. "I'm gonna go ahead and say 'How's it going' because that's what we always say. I understand it's a bit fucking stupid to ask."

Travis grunted. Jim saw the corners of his mouth twitch as if trying to smile but giving up before the expression could be realized.

"I been better." Travis's mouth barely moved. "But I'm here, man. I'm alive. You know?"

Jim moved closer. He didn't like hospitals much, and he sure didn't like good friends getting . . . what, de-eyed? He didn't like that much, either. Maybe whatever curse had fallen on Travis would fall on him if he got too close.

"That's cool." Jim shook his head, wanting to slap himself.

"I mean, that's a good way to, uh . . . to look at it."

To *look* at it? Jesus Christ, he thought. You should maybe not try to help, Jimbo, huh?

Travis's next grunt came close to taking the form of a laugh, and the corners of his mouth stayed just a little bit turned up now. "Dude. It's okay. I wouldn't know what to say either. Don't worry about it."

Relief settled in Jim's stomach. He went to the side of the bed, unsure if he should take his buddy's hand or just what. So he didn't, but he did lean on the raised side of the bed so Travis could at least sense his proximity.

"Man, I'm sorry. Just—*sorry*. I don't know what else to say. This is some fucked-up shit. What happened?"

Jim got the oddest and most disconcerting feeling that Travis's gaze slid over toward him beneath the bandages. Except Travis would never *gaze* again.

"You really want to know? Or you want the cop version?"

Jim straightened a bit. "Did you tell them something different than what happened?"

Travis moved his head about an inch to one side then the other. It finally dawned on Jim that he must have a dozen different painkillers and other meds coursing through his body.

"No. I told them everything. I told them the truth. But I know they don't believe the details."

"I don't get it."

"I told them exactly what happened. Everything I saw before I couldn't see anymore. They're not gonna argue that someone did this to me. But I know they think I was delirious or something as it happened. Dreaming, even. They think it was just some guy."

Jim leaned closer, drawn to his friend's phrasing. "You mean it wasn't?"

"Naw, man." Travis's hand lifted a bit off the sheet as if in the beginnings of a wave, then dropped again. "It wasn't just some guy. It was a dude, yeah. I mean, male. I felt his dick laying on me, I think—"

Jim's lip curled.

"—but it wasn't a normal person. You know how in horror movies no one ever believes the kids when they say there's a monster out there?"

Jim nodded. Cursed himself for trying to use body language to communicate with a blind guy. Said aloud, "Yeah."

"Well that's what this is like."

Travis lifted his right hand again, this time with dim urgency. Jim regarded it for a moment, then clasped it in his own.

Travis squeezed, not tightly, but emphatically all the same. "I'm telling you. It wasn't human. It was something else. Some monster. And it's still out there. You gotta watch Darla for me, okay? Okay, man?"

"Yeah, yeah, okay."

"No!"

Sudden strength flared in Travis's grip and Jim winced at the shock of it.

"It has claws. Or something like it. It weighs a ton, it moves quietly. It fucking *ate my eyes in front of me*. You gotta watch out for Darla and Jenny, make sure they're safe."

"Hey, hey," Jim said, putting his free hand on Travis's shoulder. "They're fine, bro. I texted with Jenny just a while ago, they're okay."

"That's not what I mean." Travis let him go. "The cops kept asking me about enemies, and drugs, gambling, debts . . . stuff like that. You know I'm not into any shady shit."

"Yeah." To Jim's knowledge, Travis was nothing but a straight-shooter who played hard ball on the basketball court and nothing more. His party days were long past, and he didn't seem to live a millionaire life on his run-of-the-mill investment banker's salary. He did okay, better than Jim, but that was all.

"So then maybe it was something else, something I forgot. I don't know. But it came for me. *Me*. It might come for the rest of my family too."

"Trav, if whoever did this wanted to hurt Darla or Jenny, why didn't he do it when he was in the apartment? Darla was right there. She's fine."

"Dunno." Travis's voice carried a stubborn edge. "Maybe it'd eaten its fill."

Jim's lip curled again. He thought of the dinner scene in *Indiana Jones and the Temple of Doom*, of Shorty and Willie stirring a soup full of eyeballs. He decided he'd skip lunch today.

"Just promise me, man."

"Dude, what the hell am I supposed to do?"

"You got a gun?"

Jim coughed. "Got one? No, I rent every so often. Trav, that's for shits and giggles, I'm not trained."

"More than me, you are."

"Trav—"

"I don't trust anyone else."

Jim blew out a sigh. "I thought you said you weren't into anything shady."

"I've known you longest. C'mon, man, we got twenty years behind us. I don't have that with anyone else. Business guys, Jenny's friends. That's it. I'm talking about my daughter's *life*."

Jim clutched the railing and took a step back, stretching

out one calf and then the other. "All right. What is it you saw?"

Travis told him. Jim decided he'd skip dinner, too, when Travis finished up.

He also reckoned the cops were most likely right. Obviously someone had attacked Trav and done some serious damage. After the trauma he'd survived, it could and almost certainly would wreak havoc with his mind, his memories. It had to have been some psycho with a penknife or, Christ, even a utensil; some nutbag with a fetish for his grandmother's collection of tea spoons from Great Britain, who the fuck knew?

But a monster? No. Not the kind Trav described anyway.

"You don't believe me."

Jim blinked. Travis had been blind for less than forty-eight hours, had he already developed some of those Marvel mutant powers to compensate?

No, Jim told himself; no, he's just being perceptive.

"I'm having trouble with it, yeah."

"That's fine," Travis said, surprising Jim. "Honestly it doesn't matter to me if you do or not. What matters to me is you keep an eye on my kid."

An eye on her? Jesus, was that a joke? No, Jim realized. Just an idiom. Travis hadn't caught it. He asked, "What about Jenny? What do you want me to do?"

Travis grunted again, not so much a laugh as a dismissal. "Sure, yeah, Jen too, whatever. Bitch."

He'd tacked it on, perfunctory. Jim smiled mildly for the first time since arriving; for the first time since yesterday when Jenny had called to tell him what had happened. She'd already been to see her ex yesterday and to take care of Darla.

Jim started to say something else, but Travis had grown

quite still, head a bit to one side, mouth again slack. He stood straight and touched Trav's shoulder.

"Trav?"

No response at first. Then Travis made some kind of noise that may or may not have been a word or two.

"I'll go," Jim whispered. "You need to take it easy."

"Jim . . ."

"Yeah, bud."

"If I'm makin' this up . . ."

"Yeah?"

"Then what did he do."

Jim tilted his head. "Do?"

"With my eyes."

Jim's mouth dried.

"Because the cops didn't find 'em. So if I'm lying or I made it up or I was delirious, that's fine. That motherfucker still took my fucking eyes with him. Who does that?"

Jim tried to get saliva back into his mouth. He wasn't successful. He patted Travis's shoulder again. "I gotta go. I'll come back later, okay?"

When Travis didn't answer, he took that to mean his friend was asleep. Jim let himself out of the room—quickly—and into the hospital hallway. He kept his pace brisk as went to the elevator and rode it down, happy to at last feel the warm Phoenix sunlight on his face.

He lifted his head and shut his eyes against the Arizona sun. For the first time in his life, he really felt the eyelids, the muscles around them, the different shades of red that played against the inside of them as he squeezed his eyes shut.

His eyes were where they were supposed to be. It was a beautiful thing.

"Fuck," Jim uttered, dropping his chin and opening his eyes again.

He got into his Jeep Liberty and took off fast.

○

"He doesn't know," Jim said while Jenny spun a mug of coffee between her fingers, scraping it against the kitchen tabletop.

"You're sure?"

"Pretty, yeah. This has nothing to do with us, whatever it is."

Jenny looked up sharply, trying to parse his words: what was the "whatever" he was referring to?

Jim sighed. "I mean, whatever attacked him, it has nothing to do with us. How is Darla?"

"Freaked the fuck out, what do you think?"

Jim bit back a response by washing his hands at the kitchen sink, turning the water on as hard and hot as he could. He loved her, but goddamn if she didn't get bitchy sometimes. Travis was right about that, and of course he'd know best.

Jim turned the water off just short of scalding himself and wiped his hands on a dishtowel hanging from the oven. "It was a stupid question, it's not what I meant."

Jenny let the spoon clang inside the mug. She rubbed her eyebrows with her fingers. "No, I know, I'm sorry. I'm the one who's freaked out. She's okay, more or less. Probably want to get her into some therapy just to be on the safe side. Jesus, can you even imagine what she saw?"

Jim nodded. He'd thought about it a lot since leaving the hospital. Seeing Travis with all those bandages, that was unsettling. Being there, in the moment, with the blood coating Travis's face and those eyeless black sockets staring but not staring right into him . . .

He kept drying his dry hands. "Yeah."

Jenny let her shoulders slump as she looked up at him

with puppy dog eyes. "Can I give you a hug?"

He tossed the dishtowel and opened his arms. Jenny went to him, holding him close. Jim held the back of her head, her dark brown hair tangling in his fingers while he pressed her into him. Yeah, that was better. Such a good fit.

"We were already separated," Jenny said, resting her cheek on his shoulder.

Jim grunted an agreement, but that was all. He'd grown tired of the refrain. He knew it himself, she didn't need to keep bringing it up. Jenny and Trav had been on the outs since . . . well, hell, since about a week after their wedding, and everyone knew it. That they'd lasted long enough to have and raise Darla into a functional pre-teen was either a miracle or an act of sheer willpower.

How *much* willpower, Jim tried not to think about. As a matter of course, fearing he'd give himself away, he never asked Trav if he'd strayed during the marriage, and he didn't ask Jenny, either. Mostly he'd forced himself to assume they had, and that it didn't matter. That was then—whenever it was—and this was now. He didn't believe in "once a cheater, always a cheater," because, goddammit, he and Jenny *weren't* cheating. The divorce had been final for months. This keeping it a secret from Trav was just . . . just friendship, really, Jim told himself. They'd tell him when—

When you're sure, Jim thought. When you know Jenny is in this for the long haul and not just a rebound. Right, Jimbo? Right?

"You sound guilty when you say that," Jim told her.

"I know. I have to stop that."

He pulled her back just far enough to allow a kiss. "You really do."

The single kiss grew to multiple, which grew to one long

mouth-to-mouth.

"I sent Darla to school," Jenny breathed, coming up for air. "I wasn't sure if I should, but she wanted to go. She said she couldn't stand just sitting around."

She kissed him again. Jim glanced at the kitchen clock over her shoulder. Two p.m. Darla wouldn't get off the bus till three.

"Is this weird though?" he asked, unbuttoning his shirt even as they continued kissing.

"I don't care." Jenny turned and leaned over the kitchen table, forearms flat across the surface, presenting her ass to him. She wore denim shorts and a yellow T-shirt, and knew he enjoyed disrobing her himself like this. "Let's not think about it. Just fuck me."

Sounded good. So he did.

Jim tried very hard not to picture Travis's bandaged eyes, watching without sight, as he banged Trav's ex-wife in their former house.

It wasn't easy.

TWO

Frank Montrose only slept a few hours a night anymore. Maybe four. Six if he was exhausted, but that was rare. An eighty-year-old man could only do so much sleeping anyway. Frank kept good tabs—just shy of a diary, in fact—of how his old-guy buddies were doing. They talked cholesterol and prostates and cancer and angina, like every aging man in the history of the United States when they gathered for pool or bocce at the senior center. Some of the guys had been in wars, but not Frank. Hell to the no, his granddaughter might say, and he'd laugh when she did. She had a mouth on her, and he approved. It drove her grandmother mad.

But Grandma Grace didn't live with Frank anymore. Their divorce had been back in the eighties, when such things were uncouth and scandalous. Frank didn't care, and knew Grace didn't either. They hated each other and hated that their parents had talked them into the marriage when she got pregnant. Good Christ, a one-week stand and then get saddled with kids and a life together when they hardly knew each other? Who thought that was a smart idea?

He didn't miss his parents much.

Frank heard the first noise just as the bad guys on *Sons of Anarchy* were starting a gunfight. Of course, in that show, who were the good guys and who were the bad wasn't easily distinguished. It was one of the reasons Frank liked it. The whole world was one big gray area, as far as he was concerned, so the anti-hero approach to storytelling made perfect sense to him. He'd been watching it well into the wee hours on The Netflix on most nights just like this.

There it was again. The sound. Muffled and cautious. Something trying to be stealthy.

He muted the TV and turned his head toward the bedroom of the little bungalow he rented. Small but neat, the tiny home lay in a renovated part of town where it once would have cost an eighth what he was paying. One bedroom, one bath, little kitchen and a tiny living room big enough for his chair and the TV. Vegetable garden in the back, grass in the front that he paid some punk kid a couple bucks to trim now and then. The place suited him fine.

But the noises . . . these were new. Not part of the usual settling that happened this late at night in a house as old as he. They'd come from the bedroom, but what were they?

Another sound.

The window, Frank thought. By God, that was the window closing. Which meant the other sounds were the window opening.

Opening then closing—to let someone in?

Frank almost called *Hello?* but realized that would be stupid if someone was actually breaking in. And—goddammit—his revolver was in the bedroom, naturally. Fuckballs.

He reached for his cell phone, laying in its usual place on the side table by his recliner, but his hand merely hovered over it. Do it, he told himself. Don't be a stupid old man, swallow your pride and call the damn police.

Except what would the boys say tomorrow when they shot pool? Ol' Frank's crossed the line, they'd josh. Ol' Frank gave up bein' a man, took his own nuts off, heh heh heh . . .

Nope. Not doing that. Hell to the no.

He carefully pushed the footrest down so the recliner was upright. He tapped the remote so the sound came back on.

Don't let them know *you* know they're here, he thought. Pretend like you decided it was nothing.

Frank stood, taking his time, just to be on the safe side. His legs were still in pretty good shape; the gardening and bocce kept him just limber enough to prevent falls, or so he hoped. He knew broken hips were all but a death sentence at his age.

Since the gun was in the bedroom, he had to find a weapon. He glanced around the room and into the kitchenette, debating using a knife. Nah . . . that seemed stupid, too easily turned on himself. Something more like a bat would be better.

His umbrella stood at a cockeyed angle in one corner near the front door. That would work. Frank shuffled to it and picked it up. It felt good and right in his hand.

Turning, Frank lowered his chin and strode purposefully toward the bedroom, heart pounding, reminding him he was still alive and still a man, by God. This sucker in the bedroom would regret choosing this old man's house to burgle.

The door was open a crack, no more. He left no lights on, so nothing spilled out. Steeling himself, Frank kicked the door open wide and poked the metal tip of the umbrella in before him.

"Get outta here, you sonofabitch!" he shouted.

The man on the bed didn't move.

Frank gasped. Real fear cascaded over his skin now—he hadn't quite believed there'd be an actual thief in the room, Jesus, this had just been a little show for himself. There wasn't supposed to be a real fucking *guy* in here.

The man on the bed wore nothing. He sat perched in the middle of the twin-sized spring mattress, looking for all the world like a hawk or maybe a gargoyle; knees bent, arms stretching down so his palms rested between his feet.

"The fuck!" Frank roared—or so he thought. The words were much more like a fart of useless sulphuric gas than an authoritative demand for answers.

The man cocked his head, reminding Frank of the chickens his parents raised. For some reason, the guy was pursing his lips halfway, making his thin lips into a small black orifice about the size of an "OK" hand signal. Apart from the backward sloping head and bald crown—and his buck-ass-nakedness—the guy had no other distinguishing features that Frank could discern in the half-light that spilled into the bedroom from the hallway.

"I—" Frank whispered.

The man sprang.

He tackled Frank into the hallway. Frank lost the umbrella along the way as the full weight of the intruder smashed into him. He heard his old ribs snapping as the attacker landed on top of him, pinning him to the tile floor.

Frank issued an involuntary groan as his head cracked against the tile. He struggled to draw breath into his bruised lungs while his assailant perched atop his prone body.

A long slow vowel sound rattled in Frank's throat as he rocked his head side to side, trying to figure out what to do first to extricate himself from this position. Goddamn the guy was heavy . . .

A hand slapped against Frank's mouth. He tried to scream in response, but his busted ribs and the guy's firm hand prevented much more than a muted moan. Frank opened his eyes just in time to see his attacker lifting his right hand as if showing Frank his fingers.

Claws, Frank saw. The guy had fucking claws. No, that couldn't be right—but yes, that's exactly what it looked like. Christ Jesus, *claws*.

And his mouth—it wasn't that he was purposefully pursing his lips. It was that this was the actual shape of the man's face. He looked as if some monstrous god had gripped his face and pulled forward, drawing all the skin down into a point within his mouth. Frank saw no teeth, just the endless black circular hole.

Frank resisted as best he could, but it was useless. Whatever this thing was, it had snapped too many ribs for him to breathe properly. Even if he could've breathed, Frank lacked the strength to shove the heavy creature off him.

Creature. Yes. No man, but a thing. An animal, maybe—some escaped bald-ass chimpanzee or great ape, maybe.

The thing pointed at Frank. Frank widened his eyes in response, trying desperately to communicate. *Yes, yes, I'll do anything you want . . .*

Sharp pain pierced Frank's left eye just at the edge of the bony socket. The creature slowly, craftily—like a demented surgeon—hooked its index finger claw into the skin and flesh there. Frank squealed under its hand, feeling the rough texture of the claw slip behind his eyeball.

The squeal became a shriek. He lost sight in his left eye. Fluid poured out of the eye socket and down his face as Frank screamed and screamed.

The thing pulled on the cords that kept his eye attached,

like it was pulling a knitting stitch tight. Then it gave one more tug that lifted Frank's head off the tile an inch or so. With his remaining eye, Frank saw the thing above him holding his left eyeball from the stalk, twirled once around its finger like a strand of spaghetti.

Frank shit himself and did not know. Piss flooded out of his penis and warmed his crotch and he did not know. All he knew was terror on a level he would not have dreamed possible before this moment.

The creature raised its hand, studying the bloody white sphere as some kind of specimen. It tilted its head back.

Don't do it, Frank thought incoherently, feeling madness beginning to edge into his consciousness. Don't you do it, don't you do it, aw Jesus, no . . .

The creature fed itself the eyeball. Frank saw no tongue pop out as it neatly stuffed the organ into its black hole of a mouth. The mangled cord dangling behind it got sucked up like a noodle a moment later. The creature chewed on it all, working its mouth like a baby on its thumb, its mouth never quite closing all the way. Something green and gelatinous dripped from its mouth and landed on the tip of Frank's nose, warm and slick.

Frank stopped screaming. Stopped breathing. There was nothing more to do but hope to die. He'd never had that thought before, this concrete desire to be simply dead because dead would be a Christ of a lot better than this hell.

The creature shook its head as if to get the last bits of food down its throat before peering down at Frank again.

It lifted its gore-encrusted finger.

No, Frank thought. No, no, no, Christ no—

New pain shot through his right eye. This time the orb was pierced directly, and the creature uttered a low, mewing sound as if disappointed. It dug around with the claw, scooping for all the viscera it could find while Frank found the wind to scream anew.

He was blind. Then the weight was gone. Frank's hoarse cries echoed uselessly in the tiny home, loud enough only to conceal the creature's departure. Frank climbed shakily to his hands and knees, puked on the tile, and tried to crawl for the living room. His hand slipped in the vomit, and he went down, chin splitting open against the tile.

He forced himself up, groaning nonsensically like a sick bovine lowing. He shuffled forward, dimly wondering if he was even going the right direction, but the sound of the TV oriented him. He was missing *Sons of Anarchy*, and now he'd miss it forever.

Frank kept going, feeling unknown fluids dripping onto the tops of his hands as he crawled. He threw up one more time and felt slick feces trailing down his backs of his thighs before crashing headlong into the side table where his phone lay.

The table crashed to the ground, taking the phone with it.

"God, God, God!" the old man chanted in a thin, reedy voice as his broken ribs threatened to puncture his lungs.

He scraped a hand across the floor, searching for the phone. At last he found it, and pulled it into his shaking hand. Frank sat up, back on his heels, feeling shit squish beneath him, and gazed sightlessly, stupidly down at the phone in his hand.

No buttons.

Just a smooth layer of plastic screen.

Frank screamed.

○

Adobe Creative Cloud crashed for the third time that morning, and Jim was about ready to take a sledgehammer to the goddamn CPU. Normally he wouldn't have put off working on the EnerJuice account—the owner was a nice guy, laid back, and trusting in Jim's skills for a great print ad—but the shit with Travis had rattled him more than he thought. He couldn't shake the feeling that it was his fault somehow; or, more correctly, his *and* Jenny's.

Guilt was a bitch, Jim decided, thumping his thumb on his desk while the computer rebooted again. He knew, functionally, that's all it was. No connection could exist between Travis's attack and Jim's relationship with Jenny. Why would *his* sin hurt Travis? That made no sense.

So maybe it wasn't that, Jim reasoned. No, not that; it's that something shitty happened to Travis on top of how shitty things had already been going.

But, Christ, they were divorced now! Sure, the motives and machinery behind the affair—*if* that's what it is, Jim corrected himself—were as trite as any made for TV movie. While Jenny and Travis had never been on the best footing, divorce and the ending of a long relationship, not to mention its effect on Darla, were still sharp and painful. Jenny was smart woman, but she wasn't excessively handy, so when the bathroom sink backed up, she'd begged Jim to come fix it if possible; she didn't have the money for a plumber, and since he and Trav had cleared a similar block two years ago in the kitchen, couldn't he just come over real quick and take a look?

Old porno music, the type that had become a staple in comedy acts, played loud in Jim's head. Bwow-chicka-bwow-bwow. The plumber is going to . . . *come* right over all right, bwow-chika-bwow-bwow . . .

Jim half laughed, half sneered. Yeah—pretty fucking trite.

He'd never married, and the ladies weren't bashing in his door lately. Maybe it was a being-forty thing. Maybe it was time to make some changes? Have a mid-life crisis? Maybe that would help. Go to the gym, buy a new car.

Sandy, his editor, knocked on the frame of the open door to his small office. She didn't look happy. Her bulk, flattered by a well-tailored suit, took up most of the doorway, pageboy haircut glimmering beneath the florescent lights.

God, now what? Jim thought.

"Jimbo. Uh . . . look, there's someone here to see you."

Shit. Jenny. Had to be. Who else was there?

Happy, though, to walk away from his CPU for a bit, he stood up. "All right. Who is it?"

"Cops."

Jim hesitated. "Cops?"

"A detective. Didn't get his name, the receptionist told me."

"Why didn't she buzz *me?*"

"Because she's a nosy little trouble-making cunt, you know that." Sandy offered a grin.

He couldn't argue. "All right. Thanks. He's in the lobby?"

"Yeah, I didn't see any reason to let him back here. Jimbo, you good? What's up? Seriously. If you tell me now I can run interference or damage control."

He came around the side of his cheap desk. "I have no idea. I haven't done anything."

Except fuck my buddy's ex-wife. Not yet a crime in this state.

She blocked his way out and made sure he met her eyes. "No shit, Jim."

"No shit, Sandy. I have no fucking clue. I'm not embezzling,

I'm not a mule, I'm not any watchlists. That I know of."

She stepped aside. "All right. But you let me know. I love ya, Jimmy."

"Love you too."

One of the many reasons he liked working here. The company was small, didn't pay what he was worth, and insisted on Windows of all goddamn things for the creative team, but Sandy ran things free but with boundaries, and kept things nice and family-like. He appreciated that.

Now on to the fucking cop, Jim thought, and walked out to the lobby.

The lobby was isolated from the cube farm in back by a single door. The lobby itself was a tiny, tiled room painted almost-white, with broad windows letting in morning sunshine. Dori, the receptionist, looked appropriately flustered as Jim walked out.

"Oh, Mr. Luxe, there's a—"

"Got the message, Dori, thanks."

By this time, the enormous black man in the gray suit had turned away from the windows where he stood and appraised Jim. Jim tried not to look too intimidated; the guy had to have played professional football in a former life. As he lumbered forward with his hand extended, though, Jim noticed a jerk in his hip that spoke of an injury of some kind. The detective could win any stand-up fight, but no way was he going to be chasing any crooks down any alleys.

"Detective Beard," the cop said. He showed credentials.

Jim shook his hand. "Jim Luxe. How can I help you?"

Beard hitched his pants. "You friends with a guy named Montrose?"

"Yeah, Travis. What's going on?"

Beard glanced at Dori. "How about we step outside for a minute?"

Jim raised his empty hands. "Just a sec, no offense, but am I under arrest here?" He didn't see any uniformed officers outside or cars in the lot.

Beard laugh gently. "No, no, nothing like that. It's just, the details might get a little gory."

Ah, shit, Jim thought. Something about the attack, of course. Though what light he could shed on it, Jim couldn't guess.

"Sure," he said, and led the way outside. He glanced back once to note Dori's fake expression of concern, which lay like a mask atop her real emotion which was frustration at being kept out of a doubtless juicy story to tell the rest of the company in the break room.

The men walked a bit down the sidewalk and stopped beneath an acacia tree that offered shade. "Is this about the attack?" Jim asked, crossing his arms.

Beard somehow nodded and shook his head at the same time. "How long have you been friends with Mr. Montrose?"

"Oh . . . almost twenty years now? Something like that."

"Mm-hmm. You ever meet the rest of his family?"

Jim tried not to hesitate too long as he considered his options. "Sure. His wife—ex-wife, Jenny. His daughter Darla. Why?"

"His mom? Dad?"

"Oh! Well. They've been broken up a long time now, if I remember correctly. I never met them. Trav didn't talk about them much, not to me."

"Past tense, huh?"

". . . I'm sorry?"

"You just used the past-tense to describe Travis Montrose."

Cocksucker, Jim thought. Bullshit TV cop show games. "Well, if I did, I didn't mean it that way. What's going on, may I ask?"

"You don't know where his folks live?" the detective asked instead of answering.

"No. In town, it sounded like, but that's it. Look, I'm sorry, I'm in the middle of designing some things right now and I'm running behind, what is this?"

Beard sighed heavily, like his job was the weight of the world. Then again, compared to being a mid-level graphic designer at a family-owned firm, maybe it was. "Mr. Montrose—senior, that is—Frank Montrose was attacked in a similar manner as his son late last night."

Jim's upper lip wrinkled up. "God. You mean the . . . like, his eyes?"

"Yeah," Beard said ponderously. "You've been to see Travis Montrose, is that correct?"

"Yes. Day before yesterday."

"So you saw the kind of condition he was in."

"Yeah." Jim unconsciously placed his palm on his abdomen.

If Beard noticed him doing it, the cop didn't comment. "Can you think of any reason someone would tear into your buddy like that?"

Jim had already spent hours thinking about that very thing, and had nothing to offer the detective. "No. Travis was—"

Fuck. Past-tense. Here he was, an innocent man, and the detective had him on the ropes.

"Travis *is* a pretty good guy. I mean, you know, he throws an elbow here and there on the basketball court, but that's about it. Plays hard. But he's a good dad, he's a good friend."

Then why are you fucking his—? *Shut up.*

Beard nodded. "Pretty athletic guy."

"I guess so. He worked out hard."

"I'm trying to imagine what kind of person could keep

him pinned down long enough to inflict those wounds."

Jim glanced down meaningfully at his own body. Travis had fifty pounds on him, handily. "You're not thinking *I* do?"

Beard gave another friendly laugh. "No sir, I do not. I also think he would've mentioned it if his assailant happened to look like a friend of his. Just checking all my bases. The fact that father and son were both assaulted the same way . . . that raises some flags. Means I need to dig around some. Might even mean Feds getting involved. Could be a cult thing, maybe. Family grudge. Dunno."

Pieces snapped into place. Jim stood up straight. "Jesus, Darla."

Beard met his eyes. "That's right. Maybe the ex-wife, too. We're a little concerned about that. One attack on one guy, well, that's an incident. Two attacks on two guys, now, that's a pattern. The same attack on two men directly related by blood . . . that's a problem."

Jim held then wiped his mouth. Goddamn. No. No, he couldn't let anything happen to that girl, and not to Jenny either. While he hadn't exactly envisioned marrying Jenny, he also hoped to still be a part of Darla's life regardless. She was a gem. Good God, he'd met her the day after she was born, when it looked like Jenny and Travis had found something to unite them. That feeling hadn't lasted, but that day, holding that baby girl for the first time—

"Is she in danger?" Jim demanded.

Beard frowned. "Impossible to say. Nothing imminent. Not that we know of. Do you have any reason to think she is?"

"No . . . no, Christ, I can't even imagine what is going on. Is someone keeping an eye on her? *Fuck* . . ." A distant piece of his brain tittered, hee hee! Keeping an *eye* on her, get it?

"She's at school," Beard said, holding up a calming hand. "And her mother's aware of the situation."

Jim blew out a breath. That wasn't enough. He'd stay the night, he'd stay every night if that's what it took. Never mind what Travis might think of it. Hell, he'd probably suggest it the next time they talked. The animosity he had toward his ex was one thing; keeping his baby girl safe was entirely another. And for fuck's sake, it's not like he wanted bad things to happen to Jenny, either; he just didn't want to deal with her anymore.

Beard scratched his head. "How, uh . . . well acquainted are you with *Mrs.* Montrose?"

Jim's nervous expression dropped, his eyes narrowing. "Why don't you ask her."

"I have. Now I'm asking you."

"What's it got to do with some psycho tearing out people's eyes?"

"Maybe nothing."

"You just get off on it, or?"

A slim smile creased the detective's face. "Getting awfully defensive, Mr. Luxe."

Jim clenched his teeth and looked away. "Fine. I'm sleeping with her. Happy?"

"Nope. I got a little girl related by blood to two men who were mutilated and blinded within the last forty-eight hours. This is what we call due diligence, making sure I've looked at every possible angle so the same doesn't happen to her."

Jim deflated. That was fair, and he knew it. "Does Travis have to know?"

"I have no reason to tell him that. Like I said—"

"Due diligence."

"Correct."

They stood in silence. Jim stared at the pebbled sidewalk, debating his next move. Beard let the silence grow before saying, "Well, I think that covers things for the moment. You should keep a close watch on the girl, call 911 immediately if anything looks out of place. Even if it feels stupid, do it anyway, that's what the cops are there for. Don't mess around with this psychopath."

"Count on it." Jim looked up. "Wait, does she know? Darla. Does she know what happened to her grandfather?"

"I couldn't say. I don't think so. That would be between her and her folks."

Jim nodded. Of course it would be.

"Thanks for your time, Mr. Luxe, I appreciate it." Beard didn't offer his hand. "I'll be in touch."

Jim waved weakly, already consumed with how to best protect Darla. He walked in the direction of the office but went past the door and on down the sidewalk, taking a right turn around the building as he pulled out his cell and called Jenny.

"Jim?"

"Jenny. How's Darla?"

Jenny sighed like she'd just sat down. "Okay. She's at school. I talked to a cop today—"

"Beard."

"Yeah, that's his . . . how'd you know?"

"He just left my office. He knows about us, FYI."

Jenny said nothing for a moment, then said, "Fine, whatever. That's irrelevant."

"That's what I said." He did not know, suddenly, if he had in fact said that to the cop, but Jenny got the message.

"Jimmy, would you come with me to get her after school? I don't want her on the bus by herself. I mean I know there'll be kids and a driver but—"

He was answering before she'd finished. "Of course, of course I will. Jenny—do you have a gun?"

"No! Of course not." The offense in her voice waned as she asked, more quietly, "Do you?"

Jim wiped the first glistening of sweat from his forehead. "No, but I'm thinking about it."

"How long would it take?"

He barked dismissively. "In this state? Hour. Two tops, I'd guess."

"But like, legal, right? You wouldn't go messing with the wrong people."

"Jesus, of course not, Jen. I'm not that stupid."

"Okay. Okay, good. Thanks."

"Have you talked to Travis? What the hell happened to his father?"

"Oh, God, Jimmy, it was the same sick thing. Whoever it was took his eyes out. And then . . . Ugh, *God*."

"And then?"

"Well," Jenny said, her voice green, "the cops couldn't find them. Just like with Travis. And he says the guy . . . you know . . ."

Jim hurried to cut her off. "But no idea who or why?"

"No."

"Did you tell Darla?"

"No, God, no. I'm not sure how. You think I should?"

Asking him a parenting question. Was that a good thing or a bad thing? Better not to think about it. There were bigger issues to worry about right now.

Still. It was nice to hear.

"Maybe not just yet. Let's you and me talk about it some more first. But I mean, whatever the hell's going on, she's going to have to stay vigilant. She can't or won't do that without knowing why. But yeah, let's talk some more later about it."

Let's. Let us. Let us both. Let us both talk and determine the best choice for your child who is not mine. Cripes.

Jim squeezed his eyes shut, then rubbed them for good measure, trying to erase the images that screened in his head, most of them having to do with Darla and the sick fuck who had an eyeball fetish. "What time does Darla get out?"

"Three fifteen."

"How far away?"

"Couple miles. A few minutes."

"I'll be there by three at the latest."

"Jimmy . . . thank you. I know you don't have to do this."

"There's nothing I wouldn't do for Darla. Period. Okay?"

"Okay. Thanks."

"You got it. See you in a bit."

They hung up. Jim stood still, letting the sun bake his scalp through his hair. He checked the time: just shy of lunch.

He wasn't hungry.

THREE

"Hey, Champ," Jim said to Darla as she climbed into the back seat of his red Jeep. He instantly felt like a douchebag for having said it.

If it bothered her, Darla didn't show it. "Hey."

Jenny turned in the passenger seat. "Hey, baby. How you doing?"

Darla let out a dramatic sigh. *"Fine."*

The adults glanced at each other. That was a pretty promising answer from a twelve-year-old. An attitude like that could only mean that things were, in fact, fine, despite the myriad crushing blows of junior high.

Jim drove them out of the parking lot.

Turning again, Jenny asked her, "You want to go visit your dad tonight?"

Jim's grip tightened on the wheel.

Darla rested her head against the window, staring longingly out at—basically anything that wasn't in this car at this moment with these people, near as Jim could discern. He didn't have kids, but he remembered being one.

Darla shrugged inside her bulky rugby jersey, a style which she'd been favoring of late. And, being fundamentally a dude in all ways, Jim had needed Jenny to explain why. He was glad he hadn't accidentally teased Darla about it. She'd never have spoken to him again. Or at least not till her early twenties.

"I'm sure he'd love to see you," Jenny pressed on.

Darla's voice was just as caustic and sarcastic as any bona-fide junior high girl. "I'm sure he'd love to *see* anything."

Jim laughed.

He did manage to catch it before it burst out of his lips, coming out instead as a rather painful snort that choked his soft palate. He coughed quickly to cover it.

Jenny spun around in her seat to face forward. When Jim looked out of the corner of his eye, he saw her pressing a fist into her mouth, her lips curling inevitably upward.

Jim let go. He let the laugh out and it was awful and wonderful. Jenny clearly took it as permission and laughed loudly with him. As he checked the rearview, he saw Darla heroically pulling her own giggle inward.

"That's *awful!*" Jenny cried through her laughter, tears toppling down her cheeks now.

When he had control of himself again, Jim shook his head. "It was necessary. Tragedy plus time and all that." He looked in the mirror again. "Thanks, Darla."

The pre-teen didn't answer, but her shoulders lurched forward a few times as she continued to suppress her laughs. Jim took that as a minor victory.

At the Montrose home—three bedroom, two bath, two car garage, nice neighborhood, mature trees—Darla beelined for her room, but did not shut the door; another good sign,

Jim decided. He and Jenny stuck to the kitchen, where Jenny started a pot of coffee and pulled a DiGiorno out of the freezer. Supreme style. She held it up.

"Sure," Jim said. "You want me to stay?"

Before she could answer, he waved her off.

"Never mind that, I'm staying, I don't much care if you invite me to or not."

Jenny set the pizza down. "I was going to say yes. I was going to *ask*."

She moved to him and hugged him warmly. Jim tensed, worried that Darla would come in and catch them, but the nature of the hug was purely nonsensual. He returned it, tightly.

"What do you think?" she whispered. "No bullshit."

He pulled away to look into her eyes. "What do you mean, about what?"

"About these attacks. Do you think someone's coming for her? Someone with a grudge against Travis and his family?"

Jim opened and closed his mouth silently a few times before settling on the imminently unsatisfactory, "I don't know."

"I know you don't, I'm asking what you think. Tell me she'll be okay."

He lowered his head to meet her gaze squarely. "I'll tell you that I'll stay here as long as it takes to find the asshole who did it. I'll tell you I'll stop at nothing to keep her safe. Okay?"

She nodded, even though her expression betrayed doubt. Doubt, or just a mother's fear—Jim wasn't sure.

He also saw an unrivaled fierceness there, burning brightly behind her gaze. One thing Travis and his father hadn't had in their favor was a mama bear's rage. No matter what hadn't gone right between she and Travis, there was no questioning either of their love for Darla.

Jim pulled her close again, squeezing her. "Come on out to the car."

"What for?"

"So I can show you something."

They parted, and Jenny sent him a questioning glance; was this a prelude to sex? Because if so, he needed to rethink that idea post-haste, her expression said. He smiled at the idea.

They exited through the kitchen door and into the garage. He guided her to the Jeep tailgate and opened it up, revealing a white plastic bag. From this he pulled a small black plastic case.

"I got this during my lunch break. It wasn't even forty-five minutes."

Jenny stepped backward. "Is that a gun?"

"Yeah. It's a, uh . . . Glock 17? I think that's what he said. Maybe 19, I forget now. With hollow point bullets."

Jenny's lip curled. "What's that mean?"

"Guy at the shop said they're designed to stop in the body. Reduces the chances of the bullet going through the target and into something or someone else." He shrugged. When he went shooting at the range—and that had been a few years ago now—he'd used what the rangemasters sold him. Full-metal jacket. Good for target practice, less good for home defense.

"You know how to use it?"

"Well, I mean, point and shoot. Like a camera."

She clearly didn't see the humor in that. Jim put the case back into the bag and shut the tailgate.

"I've shot before, it's just been awhile. There's a range up north I'd go to sometimes. We even did it in Scouts, believe it or not. Part of a safety course. Better to know how to use it than not, keeps people safer. That was the rationale, anyway."

Jenny winced up at him. "You think you could actually 'point and shoot' a person?"

Jim met her gaze. "If that person was threatening you or Darla, you're goddamn right."

He hoped he looked as confident—no, competent—as he sounded. He wanted to be a man, goddammit, but he knew that ultimately he was still just a guy who drew pretty pictures for a living and hadn't so much as run a lap in ten or more years. Naturally slender, he didn't have a weight issue to contend with, and he ate mostly okay; he avoided most fast foods these days and didn't really drink too much.

But Jenny's point wasn't beyond him. There was a world of difference between owning a firearm and being the type of guy who was good and goddamned trained to use it. Cops and soldiers, people who routinely carried, they trained for this shit over and over and over again. Blowing a few hundred bucks at the gun shop on your lunch hour wasn't the same thing.

That didn't make his promise any less valid, he told himself.

Jenny waved at the case. "Just, keep it in here for now, okay? It still makes me nervous. Bring it in tonight."

Jim dutifully put the case back. He hadn't even opened it.

He closed the gate and they went back inside. Jenny immediately called, "Darla?"

"What?" came the irritated reply.

"Just checking," Jenny said to Jim. She sighed. "This is going to be a long night."

Jim held up the DiGiorno. "Yeah, but there's pizza."

When she smiled, he felt some of his tension ease. Maybe everything would be all right.

○

The old woman had a room to herself, which was how she liked it. Laying in her bed, a knit afghan covering her frail body, Lorene knew many things: She knew the nurses didn't like her too much, she knew she didn't give a shit, and she knew it wouldn't matter for much longer.

It was an odd feeling, this dying business. What had Peter Pan said? To die will be a great adventure? Yeah, easy to say when you're eternally eleven years old. Try seventy-nine on for size, you little shit.

Lorene's skin had grown thin, and sagged even more than it had the last few years. She rarely ate anymore, and when she did, it wasn't much. Some tender fruit once in awhile, or some toast when the nurses could coax her into it. Everything and nothing hurt all at once. Each muscle complained when she moved, including her heart, which seemed to sigh with each contraction and release. It wanted a break. Fair enough, it had been going nonstop for almost eighty years. That's a long time to do one thing over and over.

Interesting, Lorene thought this night, and heard herself giggle; you'd think that would make a muscle stronger.

She wanted to roll over but couldn't quite make the shift. It took too much energy. She'd always been a tummy-sleeper but the hiatal hernia prevented that now. It could wake her up gagging, choking, feeling like she couldn't breathe. Not fun. So instead she slept on her back, propped up by a few pillows, so all the bile and acid would stay down where it belonged.

Lorene reached for her plastic water bottle and gave herself a sip. Good Lord, wasn't this just the worst? She had a TV in her private room but didn't feel like turning it on.

Nothing good on this late anyway. She could read, but that would mean wearing those heavy glasses, and the paperback brought by the late-night nurse—Shannon or Sharon or something—was a regular pocket book, not the large print Lorene generally needed.

So she lay there and thought and bitched quietly to herself, and sometimes, just sometimes, wished her son would come to see her.

Lorene gasped at the sound of something metallic near her window.

She turned her head against the cool cotton pillowcase, narrowing her eyes. What had that been? The plastic blinds were half-closed, letting in only the vaguest light from the lit walkway outside. Palm Court Community was roughly horseshoe shaped, the two-story buildings surrounding an immaculate series of paths around a stone fountain. Many of the residents took their walks there, or were wheeled around it by nurses or family members. Lorene hadn't been wheeled around it in a week now. The nurses knew how to punish bitchy old ladies.

"Hello?" she croaked. That seemed silly. Who would be at the window?

A short grinding sound pierced her ears, making Lorene take in a breath of air. It sounded like metal on concrete, like . . .

Like the bars on the windows being yanked out of their moorings.

But why would someone be doing that right now? It was past eleven at night. All the old, dying folk like her were abed, their keepers staffed down to the minimum.

A burglar.

Oh, sweet Aunt Jesus, someone was breaking in! Some rat-fuck son of a bitch was breaking into her room!

Only that made no sense either. Perhaps, if the criminal

had time and patience to search every single room in Palm Court, he might make off with a few valuable trinkets, but not much more. By the time a person lived long enough to make it to the last stand that was Palm Court Community, most of their possessions had been stripped away, sometimes already sold off by greedy grown children just waiting for Mom and Pop to kick the bucket.

So then what?

A sex criminal!

Of course. That was the only answer.

Lorene turned herself over to the right, searching half-blindly for the nurse button on the cord, just like in the hospital she'd recently been released from. Dammit, it was here somewhere. She'd never used it. Refused to use it, in fact. So of course now that she needed a hand—

The window slid open readily and silently, as if recently lubricated. Lorene turned her head and kept scrabbling for the buzzer.

"Who is it? Who are you?" she demanded in a high, wheezy voice. She wished suddenly for the cantankerous presence of Frank, who at least kept a revolver in his bed stand all his life. Now that would be something, popping this sex fiend one in the chest with a .38!

The lacy curtains split apart.

Lorene froze as a figure angled itself over the sill and slipped into her room. A man, she felt sure. Once inside he hunkered down, like a monkey, and reached up to close the curtains behind him.

Her old heart woke up now, quickly beating an emergency rhythm that she could do nothing with. Ancient adrenalin spilled into her crusty veins, motivating her to at least try to scream.

Too late.

The man leaped from the floor in one great heave, like a frog. He landed on the bed somewhat rather gracefully, from what Lorene could tell through her terrible vision and growing panic.

The old woman froze as he placed a hand over her mouth, just enough to keep any screams from being too loud. Even this close, she couldn't make out his features; her bad eyes and the dark conspired against her.

The man reached out with his right hand toward her bedside table and picked up the remote for the TV. He thumbed buttons and the screen came to life. Something British on PBS.

He turned back to her. His head moved with an odd precision that reminded Lorene of pantomimes . . . or chickens.

She moaned through his fingers, and he pressed them tighter against her. A warning. Don't scream, he was saying. Don't scream.

Lorene didn't. She didn't have the strength now. He was straddling her, knees on either side of the sheet and afghan. The bedding drew right across her body by the weight of his shins, making her blanket an effective straightjacket.

The man on top of her kept his hand pressed against her mouth, but she could breathe. Through the haze in her vision, she detected him reaching for the bedside table again.

She gasped as she felt the weight of her glasses sliding over her head.

Lorene blinked rapidly, trying to hydrate her eyes. By the blue glow of the flat screen in the corner, she could make out the man's features now.

Her old muscles locked in place, then relaxed utterly. Her

heart beat slowed suddenly into hard, heavy beats beneath her fragile ribcage.

The thing on top of her stared down, its small, circular mouth a black hole against its pale skin. It removed its hand from her mouth and peered into her eyes.

Lorene's mouth went slack. A slick of saliva dripped down her chin.

"Oh, no," she whispered plaintively as her eyebrows cinched together. "No, no, no, no. Oh, please. Oh, not you. Not you. Oh . . ."

The thing leaned close. She smelled something acidic on its breath.

It did not possess full articulation of its jaw. When it spoke, the little hole of a mouth pulsed only mildly, like a sphincter.

Its voice was soft and breathy, forcing words rather than forming them. "Ow . . . ew . . . hee . . . mee."

Wild tremors shot through Lorene's body. "Yes . . . yes I see you."

The thing nodded. It took her glasses off, gently, folded them, and placed them beside the remote. It slipped its hands beneath her head, lifting it gently off the pillows.

Still shaking, Lorene felt the creature's thin lips on her forehead, pressing down. A kiss. Its lips were dry and cracked, like her own skin.

Its thumbs rested lightly against her temples as it cradled Lorene's skull like a lover.

She wept then. "Please . . . oh, please . . . I never—"

Lorene screamed as the creature's thumbs pushed slowly into her eyes. The pressure was intense, filling her head with crushing weight. The thing took its time with her, pushing, pressing, until first her left then right eyeballs ruptured.

Lorene sucked in a scorching breath, which then parked uselessly in her lungs. She stopped breathing entirely. Her near-blindness was now complete. Half-mad with pain and fear, she still felt the thing's claws now digging into her eye sockets. The tips scraped around the edges of bone, like a kid scooping every last bit of ice cream from a bowl.

A slender expulsion of air came from Lorene, a tire losing pressure. The weight of the thing above her shifted. She felt its almost bald head beside hers as it let go of her. She sank slowly back into the pillows as her lungs expelled their last in one long near-silent gasp.

But she heard. She heard it all. As the creature hovered over her, its smooth, dry cheek beside her own, its mouth by her ear, she heard.

It chewed slowly. The mouth was clearly open, the inner workings of its maw seeming to savor each squelch as it consumed her eyes.

It wanted her to hear. It wanted her to know.

Lorene heard it swallow. One damp, cat-vomit pulse.

Then it breathed on her, gave her another kiss on the temple, and then the weight was gone.

Lorene Montrose did not take another breath.

O

The sex was perfunctory, Jim thought. Good, as always, but not . . . *there*. First of all, Darla was asleep down the hall, that was one thing. Not enough to stop Jenny's advances or make him turn her away, but still. The knowledge creeped him out a bit. Christ, what if she walked in? But the door was closed and locked, and Darla had crashed by about eleven, and it seemed clear she wasn't apt to rise any time soon.

Jenny had closed her door quietly, then turned to Jim in the hall and taken his hand.

They'd said nothing, just walked into her bedroom, shut the door, and immediately fell into each other's bodies, kissing, groping, sighing roughly in one another's ears. When the last piece of clothing hit the floor, Jenny reached out and flipped the doorknob lock, and that was it. They'd fallen into the king-size bed, right on top of the comforter.

Jim had pressed his lips together hard as he came, feeling like all the stress and worry of the last couple of days was exploding out of him in several exquisite pulsations. By the time he was done and collapsing on top of her, he already knew Jenny hadn't come, despite the fact that she'd gripped the wrought iron headrest behind her as if bracing, but she didn't comment on it and didn't seem to care. She just pulled herself closer to him as he rolled onto his side, and held him close.

Then the doorbell rang.

Jim tightened and sat up fast. Jenny followed suit.

"What the hell?" he barked, and looked at the clock. Nearing one.

Jenny clutched his arm. "What if it's *him!*"

Jim got the implication instantly. They parted, sliding off the bed, stumbling into their clothing. The gun, goddammit, the gun was still in the fucking Jeep!

The doorbell rang again.

Jim held up a hand as Jenny flicked on the bedside light. "Wait, wait, wait. He wouldn't ring the bell."

"We don't know!" Jenny snapped, and raced from the room into the hallway.

Barefoot, Jim followed as she opened Darla's door. The girl lay sprawled at an angle across the bed, her oversized nightshirt twisted around her torso.

Jenny breathed out and shut the door again. "Let's go see."

Jim nodded. They crept to the front door. Jim peered into the spyhole—and dropped his shoulders.

"Shit," he said, and opened the door.

Detective Beard stood beneath the porch light. His face was grim.

"Mr. Luxe," the cop said, and raised his eyebrows a bit as if peering over Jim's shoulder. "And Mrs. Montrose?"

Jenny came around Jim's side, arms around her middle. "I haven't changed it yet," she muttered, then to the cop said, "What's going on?"

"Everything all right here?" Beard asked.

The two traded worried frowns. "Yes," Jim answered. "We just checked on Darla, she's safe and sound. What is it? It's one o'clock in the goddamn morning."

Beard nodded as if that's what he either was expecting to hear—or just hoping. "There's been another attack. Travis Montrose's mother."

Jenny bit her lower lip and pressed herself into Jim's shoulder. Jim gripped a handful of his own hair in one hand. "Are you serious?"

A stupid question at one in the morning while talking to a police detective, but the cop clearly didn't mind.

"Yes, I'm afraid so. Felt like coming by here might not be the worst idea, you know."

Jenny peeked up. "Was she killed in the . . . *same* . . .?"

"The same manner, yes, it appears that way. If there was any doubt about this being all connected to the Montrose family, that doubt has passed. The FBI is getting involved now."

"Oh, God," Jenny groaned before Beard finished, and turned to Jim again.

"Have you told Travis or his dad?" Jim asked, choking a bit on how dry his throat had become.

"Not yet, they're both still recovering in the hospital. We'll tell them in the morning. That's another little part of what brings me out here right now. I'm a dad myself, so . . . it might be better, Mrs. Montrose—"

"Jenny," she said, pulling herself up. She stood tall now, but kept Jim's hand clasped in her own.

"It might be better, Jenny, if you were there with Travis when we told him," Beard said. "A thing like this, he's going to need someone familiar around. Plus there's his daughter, he'll want to know she's all right, I assume."

"Yeah," Jim said before Jenny could. "He'll *need* to know that."

"How about we meet at the hospital around ten," Beard said, and it wasn't a question.

Jim turned to Jenny, who nodded tightly. "That would be fine."

"All right. I'll see you there." The detective turned.

"Uh, sir? Are you leaving anyone here overnight? A police officer?"

Beard shook his head. "No, we can't really leave a uniform here, but I will make sure there's a cruiser coming by as often as possible. Keep your phones on and ready to dial if there's an emergency, we'll be here right quick."

"Okay. Thank you."

Beard turned once more, but hesitated. "You two folks have been home all night, I assume?"

"Aw, *Jesus!*" Jim spat. "You know what—?"

Jenny squeezed his hand. "Jimmy, don't. It's all right. Yes, detective. We've been here at the house since a little after three with my daughter. Would you like me to go and get her?"

Beard waved. "No, that won't be necessary. Sorry for the bad news and disturbance. I'll see you at ten."

"Good night," Jenny said, closing the front door as Jim stewed in the entryway.

"The nerve of that fucker!" he said in a harsh whisper once the latch was closed. "Can you even—"

"*Shut up,*" Jenny barked.

Jim froze.

"You shut up and listen to me," Jenny went on, pointing a finger at him. "Someone is out there killing or trying to kill every member of my daughter's family. And until this is over, I will cooperate fully and completely with anything the police want to investigate, do you hear me?"

Jim nodded quickly. It was all he could do.

"Good," Jenny said. "I'm going to go lie down and try to sleep, knowing that I goddamn won't, so that I can get up in the morning and tell my ex-husband his mother is dead. I'd appreciate it if you'd stay up and make sure nothing happens to my child."

She turned and marched down the hallway and into the bedroom, opening Darla's door on the way and leaving hers open as well.

Jim gazed down the length of the dark hall for a long moment, then went into the garage and got the Glock.

FOUR

Jim stayed up the entire night. He loaded and unloaded the Glock a dozen times, and checked the locks on the doors twice that. He alternated between standing at the living room windows and the kitchen windows, his eyes drying out over the course of the night, until the sun finally rose and Jenny came out.

"Anything?" she asked.

"No. Did you sleep?"

"A little. Not much. You?"

"No."

Jenny's shoulders drooped. "You really didn't."

"That's what I said." And he was pissy enough to prove it.

"Go lay down," Jenny urged. "I'll get breakfast for Darla."

He wanted to fight, something petty and immature, but in the end he was too damn tired to do it. He walked past her to the bedroom just as Darla poked her head out of her room.

"Oh! Hey, Jim." She said it with her eyes half-closed in the manner of all just-woken adolescents. She didn't seem surprised. Jim didn't know what to make of her lack of surprise at seeing him.

"Hey, Darla. Sleep okay?"

"Uh . . . yeah. Did you? I mean, did you sleep over?"

Sleep over. The juvenile term made something in his heart bend backwards. Yeah she was twelve, and twelve was still just a kid, a *little* kid at that. She probably hadn't even meant to say it like that.

He very nearly touched her cheek, but resisted. Darla was not his kid. She was Travis's. His best friend Travis.

That thought brought the morning into stark relief: he and Jenny had a shit job to do today, and part of it was going to have to include telling Darla that her grandmother was gone and her grandfather was blinded just like her dad. Oh, and that the cops were worried she might be next.

He reached out and tousled her hair. She let him. "Yeah, I slept over. Your mom and dad wanted me to stay."

The words came frighteningly easy. Was it a lie? Half a lie? No, he decided. Once Travis understood the stakes, he'd be grateful as hell that Jim had stayed overnight. Overnight and awake with a Glock, to be specific. Yeah, he'd appreciate that.

"Because of what happened to Dad?"

"Yeah," Jim said, trying to sound matter of fact. He blinked his eyes blearily. His eyelids felt like fine-grit sandpaper. "You want to go see him this morning?"

"Maybe." Darla slid down the hall, scratching her head with both hands.

Jim couldn't tell if that was a yes, a no, or an actual maybe. Well, the hell with it, that would be between her and her mother. He went on into the bedroom, shut the door, and fell face-first into the mattress. He slept with scent of Jenny's lavender body lotion tickling into his nose.

○

Darla went.

They took the Jeep again. Jim crammed a three-hour nap in before being roused by Jenny. She looked put-together but not over-dressed. Darla, naturally, had chosen a green and white striped rugby shirt that may as well have been a dress in its own right. Jim had brought no extra clothes, and so contented himself with a few splashes of water on his face and treating everyone to Starbucks on the way. His Americano was hot and bitter and perfect, scalding the night's terrors from his entire body as the too-hot water rushed down his throat.

There hadn't been time or opportunity to converse with Jenny about how Darla thought the day was going to go. What did she think she was going to see? To hear? Well, they'd find out soon enough. He wasn't sure he liked the idea of surprising her, but he also wasn't about to bring it up now. Darla, no matter how much he cared about her, was simply and utterly not his. He was not her dad, he was not even a blood relative. However Jenny wanted to handle things that was up to her, and he'd support it. As best he could, anyway.

All was fine until they reached Travis's hospital room door.

Darla planted her feet on the slick tile. Her body locked up like she'd hit an invisible wall.

"No."

She stated it without hysterics or attitude. Just a fact. Nope, she was not walking through that door.

"Hon," Jenny said, "it's your dad, he'll want to know you're okay."

Darla took a step back, eyes locked on the pale wood door. "Then tell him. I'm not going in there."

Jim put a hand on her shoulder. "What is it, D?"

She shook her head. "I don't want to see him like that. I can't. I can't do it."

Jim met Jenny's eyes over Darla's head. *Flashbacks?* he tried to mouth. Jenny only shrugged quickly. He tried to mouth the letters P-T-S-D but gave up, feeling foolish.

"Okay, hon," Jenny said. "It's up to you. If you don't want to go in, that's fine. But I *do* need to go in, and I can't have you out here by yourself."

"I'll stay," Jim said, catching the hint. He was surprised to sense relief in his belly. He didn't want to go in, either, but didn't know it until he no longer needed to. "We'll grab a seat in the hall over there."

Jen nodded. "Okay. Thanks, Jim. Darla, if you change your mind, just come on in, okay?"

Darla nodded and broke for the central nurses' station, situated like a hub from which four hallways extended like spokes. Jenny touched Jim's arm in thanks before letting herself into the hospital room, gently saying Travis's name.

Jim followed Darla to the hub and sat down on a padded bench beside her, leaning his head against the wall. He sipped his coffee. "Want anything?"

"No, thanks."

"How you doing? Really."

Darla sighed theatrically, but Jim sensed sincerity in it. Understandably. After what she'd seen in her room that night, she had a right to feel put-upon. Hell, she didn't even know about her grandparents yet; how would she stomach *that* information?

"I mean, okay, I guess," Darla said. She pulled her legs up to sit cross-legged on the bench in a maneuver Jim hadn't been to accomplish in twenty years. Fuckin' kids, he thought with affection.

Darla ran her forearm under her nose as if it were leaking. "I keep . . . *seeing* it."

Jim pulled away from the wall. "Seeing your dad?"

She nodded.

"Hey, that's totally understandable," he said. "That was a hell of a thing to go through."

"Not as bad as what happened to him."

"No, but . . ." He waffled. How to handle this? Darla was confiding in him, and he didn't want to ruin it. He took a deep breath and dove in. "Look, the thing is, when something bad happens to someone else, that doesn't invalidate how you feel about it. Or how you react. You know? When 9/11 happened, lots of people who were not anywhere near New York developed panic attacks and PTSD symptoms. That was real for them. And they were allowed to feel those things. No point in pretending they didn't feel that way. Does that make sense?"

Darla nodded again, her expression nominally thoughtful. Mostly, Jim thought, she looked guilty. For not having been hurt, and/or for not being in the room right now with her dad. Hell, maybe even for some lingering doubts over the divorce. He knew it fucked kids up in one way or another, or so he'd read. Things between Trav and Jenny had been bad, but never abusive, not that Jim ever heard. It wasn't one of those situations where the kids breathe a sigh of relief now that the trauma is finally over. No, theirs had been one of those "we just don't fit" type breakups, and Jim wondered if those were harder on the kids than the other kind.

The elevator dinged across the room from them, and Detective Beard stepped out. He caught Jim right away, and ambled over. Jim suddenly wondered if the cop ever changed his suit, if he only had the one, or if he just looked the same no matter what he was wearing.

"Morning," Beard said with an invisible hat tip. "This must be Darla."

Darla looked up at him, squinting. She did not ask the obvious question, so Beard answered it himself.

"I'm Detective Beard," he said to her. "I'm in charge of the case involving your dad."

"Did you find someone?" Darla's voice was frighteningly adult, Jim thought.

"Well, no, not yet, but we are working on some leads."

Jim blinked. Was that true, or was the cop being patronizing? He couldn't tell.

Beard gestured to him. "You mind if I talk to Mr. Luxe for just a minute?"

Darla turned to Jim, her face questioning. Jim pointed down the hall. "Just over there. I'll still be able to see you."

Now Darla's expression turned to youthful contempt. "Why does that matter?"

Shit, Jim thought. He'd played that wrong. *She doesn't know she might be in danger. She has no reason to think that, so I just look like an overprotective goon.*

He forced a smile. "Right. Sorry. We'll just be a couple minutes. Think about if you want anything else to eat, okay?"

Darla managed to shrug, nod, and shake her head all at the same time in the way only kids know how to do. Jim rose and followed Beard down one of the hallways, out of Darla's earshot.

"Was that true?" Jim asked right away. "You've got some leads?"

"We have, uh . . . something." Beard cleared his throat. "Is Mrs. Montrose here with you?"

"She's talking to Trav. Telling him about his parents, I

believe. I'm not sure. Darla didn't want to go in, so we were waiting out here."

"And he—Travis Montrose, he never talked about any brothers? Sisters?"

"No. He's only child."

Beard nodded a bit. "What room's he in?"

"Three twenty-four." Jim pointed. "What exactly's happening?"

"I'm not sure, Mr. Luxe. I need to talk to Mr. Montrose right now."

"Can I come?"

"Doesn't matter to me, that'd be up to Mr. Montrose."

Jim glanced quickly at Darla, who sat typing and swiping on her phone. "Let me just check in with her."

Beard indicated his willingness to wait. Jim jogged to Darla and crouched in front of her.

"Listen, I'm going to go with the detective in to see your dad, okay? You'll be okay out here?"

"Where better than a hospital for something bad to happen to me."

Her angsty sarcasm was rather refreshing. He half-grinned and said, "Okay. I'll be right back. Stay here."

Darla gave no indication she heard or that she would obey him. He figured it was the best he'd get. He returned to Beard, and the two men walked to Travis's room.

Jim went in first. Jen sat by the bed, but was not—as Jim discovered he'd been expecting—holding his hand or touching Travis any way.

Travis lay on his back just as Jim had seen him previously. He thought the bandages around his head were fresh; bright white and lacking stray strings. His mouth was set, jaw clamped tight.

"Trav? It's Jim, man."

Travis gave no indication of having heard. Jenny faced him, and while she was not weeping, her face was strained. She'd definitely told him.

"There's a cop here to see you," Jim went on, approaching the bed. "Is that okay, man? I can tell him to go."

Travis turned his head side to side, minimally.

"He can stay?" Jim asked, to clarify.

"Sure," Travis croaked. He sounded like he needed water badly.

The detective introduced himself and approached the opposite side of the bed. "Has your ex-wife told you what's happened?"

"Yes."

Jim thought he saw Travis's jaw trembling, but wasn't sure. He crossed his arms.

"Your mother and your father?"

"Yes. Is my dad still alive?"

"He is. He'll recover, ultimately, it sounds like."

"But not with any eyes."

Travis's voice was a monotone, and reminded Jim somehow of the flatline of a heart monitor.

Beard sniffed as if unsure how to respond. He let the comment pass. "Mr. Montrose, your father isn't being particularly helpful with his own case. I'm sure you can appreciate that we have some concerns about your daughter's safety."

"Darla!" Travis barked, sitting up in bed. "She's here, she's safe, right?"

"She's right outside," Jim said quickly. "She's fine, man."

Travis stayed up on his hands for a moment, breathing hard, before slowly letting himself back down to the pillows.

"Your father did say one thing that struck us as a little strange," Beard went on once Travis was settled. "Then he clammed up. What can you tell me about your brother, Mr. Montrose?"

Jim reared back, looking at Trav as if Trav could betray something with a look in his eyes. Travis went stolid again, mouth set in a grim line.

Jenny glanced at the cop, at Jim, and then back to her ex. "Travis? What's he talking about?"

"You think it's him?" Travis asked the cop.

"Who him?" Jenny demanded, her voice edging toward shrill.

"I didn't recognize him . . . it's been so long, I thought he was dead, I hadn't thought about him in ages."

"Travis?" Jenny said. "What are you talking about?"

Travis's mouth twitched. "I don't know his name."

He said this so quietly, with such the barest movement of his lips, that Jim wasn't sure he'd even heard correctly. But Beard leaned a little closer and Jenny leaned a little further away so—yeah. He heard it.

"What?" Jenny whispered. "Travis—"

"We were twins. But something was wrong with him."

Jim felt his stomach twist, and laid a palm across his belly. Wherever this story was going, it wasn't going to end well.

"I don't know what. Physical. Mental. Both. Mom and Dad tried to help him at first, I think. When we were little. But they couldn't do it. Aw, Jesus . . ."

"What happened, Mr. Montrose?" Beard asked. His voice sounded kind, but Jim didn't believe it.

Travis was breathing hard now, chest rising and falling rapidly. It reminded Jim of how he sounded after a basketball game, but there was a different quality to it. It wasn't the healthy gasping of a forty-something guy keeping tabs on his heart by shooting hoops. It was the terrified breathing of an animal, trapped.

"They had to keep him in a room," Travis said through his teeth. "They couldn't control him. Piss and shit everywhere. *He was a fucking demon.*"

Jenny brought her hands to her mouth, stifling a sound. Jim winced.

"Never had a name," Travis said, easier now, like he'd said the worst of it. "Just 'your brother,' that's all they'd call him. Go take this up to your brother, go hose down your brother—"

Travis stopped short, as if catching the terrible admission he'd just made. *Hose* him down? Jim thought, and glanced at Beard to see if he'd heard it.

He had. The cop's eyes glinted in the florescent light above Travis's head, and then Jim fought to choke down an insane giggle: what did Travis need an overhead light for?

Maybe you should go, he told himself. Maybe you should just sit tight out there with Darla and not listen to all this.

But Darla was the very reason he needed to stay. He'd already jumped to a conclusion, and he was sure Beard was there already too; *had* been at that conclusion before he got here. Of course.

"Brother" had come home. But from where?

"Where is your brother now, Mr. Montrose?"

Travis shook his head against the pillows. "I don't know. They took him away eventually. I was nine, maybe ten."

"You were *both* nine or ten," Beard clarified, and Jim thought, *You bastard.*

"Yes. I guess we were."

"They took him away—to where, did you say?"

He *didn't* say, Jim thought, and again lowered his estimation of the cop. He seemed to be enamored of his own authority, cribbing lines from fucking cop shows.

"I *don't know*," Travis emphasized. "I asked once, when I noticed it was quiet in the room, and my dad smacked me across the face. He said, 'We don't ever talk about him, never again.' So I didn't. After a little while . . . he just never existed."

"Jesus," Jenny whispered, now covering her eyes instead. "How could you not tell me that?"

Jim knew the answer. He was surprised Jenny didn't know or guess, but then maybe it spoke to why they were exes instead of married. Frank Montrose was a sonofabitch, that was why. Whether he'd always been that way or because of this second child he'd abandoned—and worse—Jim didn't know, but he knew from how Travis talked about him right now that, yeah . . . Travis was still in some way afraid of his old man.

Travis didn't answer her. "You think it's him? You think it's my brother?"

"Can't say for sure, of course, but it's something I'm going to follow up on."

"Ya think?" Jenny snapped at the cop. "Jesus Christ! Some fucking freakshow is out there hurting and killing the members of his family, which might very well include my daughter! How about you get the fuck out there and detect some shit, huh?"

"I'll, uh, go check on Darla," Jim said before Beard could respond. He let himself out quickly.

Holy fucking *shit*, he thought as he walked briskly down the hall toward the nurses' hub. That is a goddamn horror show is what that is. Good God. It sounded like some real

V.C. Andrews type shit.

So what had happened to "Brother?" he wondered. What was wrong with him? What did they do to him? Or *with* him for that matter? Clearly, as far as Jim was concerned, whatever the Montrose couple had chosen to do with the kid, it hadn't worked.

If this was him. That was the most obvious choice, but still . . . what has to happen to a human being to make him search out and mutilate the members of his own—

"Darla?"

Jim stopped dead in front of the nurses' desk. The girl wasn't sitting on the bench.

He turned to the nurse behind the desk. "Excuse me, did you see where the girl sitting here went?"

The nurse looked up, at the bench, then around the circular room. "Uh . . . elevator."

"She *left?*" He said this while bolting for the elevator doors. "Up or down?"

"I don't know. Down?"

"Ah *fuck!*" He stamped on the down button.

"Sir, I need you to please keep your—"

The elevator dinged and opened. The car was empty.

"Fuck off!" he growled, leaping inside and thumbing the ground floor button.

He raced from the cab as soon as it opened, startling two elderly women who looked like sisters. Jim muttered an apology and turned left for the cafeteria. That made the most sense, he told himself; she'd gotten hungry. Sure.

It took less than a minute for him to pace between the tables and scan the entire room. Not here. He cut in front of the checkout line and gave a cashier her description; no luck.

Swearing again, Jim went into the lobby and stopped in the

middle, glaring all around. He tried the gift shop; nothing. He covered as much of the ground floor to which he had access, then took his search outside.

Darla was gone.

FIVE

Jim walked a lap around the hospital grounds, scanning in all directions. He took his phone out and let his thumb hover over Jenny's number; he didn't have Darla's or else he'd have called her himself. Now he'd have to bring Jenny in. He tried not to think of the consequences of such a choice, desperately wanting to find the girl himself first.

But no. Either he'd passed her in his haste somewhere, or Darla was well and truly gone.

By herself or not—that was the real question.

Jim paused as he reached the lobby doors after his route around the building. Okay, he thought. Okay, if some mutant psychopath had shown up and grabbed her, *most likely* the nurse would have mentioned that, right? Right. Okay. So she left of her own accord.

Sure, he thought, going back inside and aiming for the elevator. She's a young girl still, and she's been through a lot, just like you told her yourself. She wanted to take a walk or . . . or go to the mall or whatever it was twelve-year-old girls did when they were freaking out. Maybe she had a friend nearby.

Sure. Any number of scenarios were possible. Perfectly reasonable, safe scenarios.

But he had to have Jenny call her.

Jim pulled back from the elevator bank at the last second, figuring he may catch Darla coming back inside or even coming out of one of the elevators; bunching up in the third floor wasn't going to help.

He tapped Jenny's button. She answered after two rings. "Jim?"

"Hey, listen, Darla took off."

"*What?*"

Shit. "Yeah, I went out to the hall and she was gone. The nurse said she got into the elevator. I've been all over the grounds, inside and out, I can't find her. Can you call her?"

"Jesus," Jenny spat, and the line died.

Jim pinched the bridge of his nose. My thoughts exactly, sweetie.

He moped outside again, thinking if Darla was inside the hospital still, she'd end up back where she belonged without his help. If she'd left the building, maybe he could catch her coming in.

Because she has to come back, he thought as he turned right out of the lobby, headed for the downtown area. Lots of shops and restaurants that way, maybe she'd wanted to get something substantial to eat, and the thought of hospital food turned her stomach.

He was right.

Jim stopped short as he turned a corner, spotting the wayward pre-teen on a public bench outside an olive oil store. Darla sat with her arms wrapped around her middle, leaning forward as if about to puke.

Jim approached carefully, like approaching an off-leash

unfamiliar dog. Then he paused and thumbed a quick text to Jenny—*Found her she's fine call you soon*—before slipping his phone into his pocket and continuing his approach. He got to within ten yards before speaking.

"Hey, Darla."

She didn't look up, but he could tell she heard him just fine. She made no move to bolt, so Jim slid onto the bench beside her.

"Yeah, you scared the crap out of me," he said as if picking up the middle of a conversation. He wanted to add, I fucking told you to stay where the fuck you were goddammit! but sense won out and he kept his mouth shut.

"I'm sorry," Darla whispered after a moment. "I shouldn't have even come."

Feeling a bit more in control, Jim relaxed against the bench. "What makes you say that?"

"I don't even like them."

"Like who?"

"My parents, dude, who else?"

Jim felt his phone buzz, and ignored it. It would be Jenny. Speaking of which:

"You got your phone?"

"Yeah, I'm not answering it right now."

"Your mom's going to freak out."

"Oh, well, there'd be a change of pace."

Jim snorted. The noise brought a quick glance and quicker smile from the girl, both of which were gone a heartbeat later.

He let the silence grow. The important thing was she was safe. If Darla wanted to confide any more, that would have to be up to her.

"I mean, it's not like I'm glad he's hurt," Darla said.

Jim nodded.

"But also like, maybe he had it coming, you know?"

He thought about Brother, and wondered if she was right. Granted, he'd been not much older than Darla herself when . . . when what? How had the Montroeses dealt with Brother, anyway? Maybe it was best not to know.

"Divorce is shitty," Jim said. "No way around it."

"Yeah." Darla sniffed. "I guess I should go back, huh?"

"I think so, before your mom sends the brute squad."

She met his eyes, wrinkling hers. "What's that?"

Jim grinned and stood. "Have you not seen *The Princess Bride?*"

She followed him up. "No, what's that?"

"Oh, D. We have a lot to show you. Maybe tonight, even. Come on, let's head back."

She nodded glumly and allowed herself to be led back to the hospital. Jim nearly put an arm around her shoulders, but didn't. Jesus, navigating this whole not-his-own-kid thing was getting to be a hassle.

Now that she was accounted for, Jim noticed the adrenalin rushing through his body He was ready to attack, and only slowly was that feeling dissipating. If Travis's fucking brother showed up, he'd have to get through Jim first.

It won't come to that, Jim told himself as they reached the lobby doors.

It won't.

SIX

Jim, Jenny, and Darla piled out of Jim's Jeep two hours later with bags of burritos from a local place that was usually one of Darla's favorites. Jim was unconvinced she could be bought off so readily, but didn't argue with Jenny, who was still steaming about her disappearance and Jim's inability to keep tabs on her.

"Dar?" she said now as they slammed the Jeep's doors. "Listen, hon, after we eat, we need to talk, all right?"

"About what." A statement. Darla wasn't having it.

"About a lot of things," Jenny said with a warning note. "Just humor me, Darla."

Darla shrugged carelessly and let herself into the house. She was in her room, the door closed, by the time Jim and Jenny had come in and closed the door behind them.

"Fun stuff," Jim said, setting his burrito on the table.

Jenny slammed herself down in a chair and rubbed her eyes. "Christ, Jim. I need a Xanax or something, those are the stress pills, right?"

"I think so." He took out the rest of the food and spread

it out in front of her. "So what'd Beard say, what happens next?"

Jenny sighed and picked up her burrito. It was fully half the size of her head. "We don't have anything to worry about, or at least that's what *he* says. This . . . brother of Travis's is showing a ritualistic pattern, he said. Just going after the people he thinks harmed him. Or, probably did, I should say. He and the FBI think it's, quote, 'very unlikely' he'll try to hurt Darla."

"Or you."

"Yeah, or me."

"You don't look convinced."

Jenny finished a healthy bite. "Jim, my mother-in-law is dead. Travis's brother, her own son, who I didn't even know goddamn existed until this morning is the one that killed her. Travis and his dad are recovering from a—what did Beard call it—a life-altering violent crime. The fucking Feds are involved, Jim! You're goddamn right I'm not convinced."

She tossed the burrito down and sat back, crossing her legs and bouncing her foot.

"Sorry," he muttered. He was still hungry but set his own burrito down too. A show of solidarity, or so he hoped. "What can I do?"

"You can watch my fucking daughter next time!"

Jim lowered his gaze, deciding he had this coming and he may as well take it. Jenny ranted at him for a full five minutes, and Jim was sure Darla heard it all. He only nodded and offered the occasional "You're right" or "I know" to let her know he was listening.

And he *was* listening—he felt like shit, he felt like an asshole . . . he felt like an asshole shitting, for that matter.

He figured she was done when she took another bite of

her burrito. Jim blew out a breath and took one of his own. They chewed in silence.

"I'm so sorry," Jim said at last. "You're absolutely right, and it won't happen again, I swear to you. I love that kid, you know that, right?"

Jenny rolled her eyes first, nodded her head second.

"Do you want me to stay tonight?"

"Yes." While Jenny's face showed frustration, her response came instantly.

"All right. What about telling her about her grandparents? You want me here for that or not so much?"

Jenny continued eating, eyes drifting thoughtfully around the kitchen before answering. "No. I'll do it. Do you need to grab some clothes and whatnot?"

"Yeah, I probably should." He finished his meal and crunched the paper in between his hands. "I'll do that now, take my time. She's expecting you to talk to her about something anyway."

"Yeah. Jesus, Jim, what a goddamn nightmare."

He stuffed the trash into the kitchen garbage and put a hand on her shoulder. "It is, it really is. But they'll catch him. Everything will be okay."

"Who's going to take care of Travis?"

Jim jerked, and hoped it didn't transmit down his hands and into Jenny's shoulders. "I don't know. I mean, I'll help him, of course. But he won't be an invalid, either, Jen. Being blind isn't the end of the world."

"Easy for you to say."

"True."

Where was this headed? Good God, she wasn't going to take him back after all this, was she? Blind or not, they weren't a good match. Jesus, what if she got it into her head to pity fuck him? Oh shitballs, what a mess *that* would be . . .

"I should go." He lifted his hands and patted his pants for his keys. He hoped she'd say something affirming, something like Hey, don't worry about us, we'll still be together. Only she didn't.

"See you tonight," he said quickly, and let himself out.

○

Jim came back at six bearing Chinese food. Whether he should do so or not was the first text he sent Jenny since leaving. She'd replied with a thumbs-up emoji and nothing more. That was the moment he felt it; felt the door shutting on their little tryst. He told himself he was being hypersensitive; then that he was being *in*sensitive; then that he was being premature. It hadn't been the best week for her family after all, and who knew how Darla was dealing with the information Jenny had to give her that day. No, probably Jenny was just exhausted and a thumbs-up was all she could reasonably manage.

He made that his mantra. The alternative soured his stomach. But he'd felt it before, back in high school and college; the somehow inevitable snap of a relationship ending. Something he saw in their eyes, or the way messages became terse or outright unresponsive. That's what that little brown thumb felt like.

Jim let himself into the house. He found Darla parked in front of the TV, a pillow crunched against her torso, knees draw up. On the screen, rich white twenty-somethings pretending to be teenagers tried to stop an evil supernatural event.

"Hey, D. Hungry?"

She didn't answer. Her expression reminded him of someone completely stoned.

He set the bags on the coffee table. "D? You okay?"

"Pretty much not okay, dude."

Jim sat down on the far end of the couch. "Where's your mom?"

"Bathroom. Shower."

"Did she, uh . . . how'd, how'd the talk go?"

"You mean did she tell me my grandmother was dead and my grandfather had his eyes ripped out just like my dad? Yeah. It was lovely, thanks for asking."

Jim let the sarcasm glide off him as best he could. "Were you close to them?"

"Psh. No. They were assholes."

"Yeah, that's kinda what I heard, too. Are you scared?"

Darla pulled her eyes away from the screen and lit them on him. "What do you think?"

"I don't know, D, that's why I'm asking. I'm trying to be helpful over here, to you and your mom."

"And that includes boinking her?"

Jim made a noise, some cross between a laugh and a groan and a gasp. "Wh-what makes you say that?"

The derision in her gaze said it all. Jim's shoulders slumped. "I have, like, literally nothing to say right now."

Darla turned back to the TV, studying the used car commercial as closely as she had the show. "I don't care. Go for it. Whatever."

He gambled. "I don't think you mean *that*. That you don't care."

"Well what should I say, dude? 'Stop?' You're grown ups, you do what you want no matter what I say, so, have fun. Have a *baby*."

That time he did laugh, because the thought was absurd,

but the laugh fell from his mouth with the weight of a bowling ball.

"That's not in the plan, D."

She shrugged.

Jim pulled her seared shrimp out of the white plastic sack and set it on the table in front of her, then added napkins and a fork. The rest of the bag he bunched up into a handle as he stood.

"Can I tell you something? If you really did say stop, I would. I *will*. You're more important."

He walked out, feeling very dramatic and adult. The sensation passed by the time he reached the kitchen ten feet away—by then he just felt like a dick. Literally and metaphorically, just a big dick.

Jenny came walking in, barefoot and naked except for a large bath towel wrapped around her body, and a second hanging from her head like a new crop of hair. "Hey."

"Hey," Jim muttered back, and unpacked the sack. "Darla knows."

"Darla knows what? About her grandparents? Yeah, we talked earlier. She took it okay I think."

"About *us*."

Jenny froze, peering at him as if from under a wizard's hood. Her voice hissed from the darkness of it. "You told her about us?"

Jim kept his voice low. "Christ, no. She figured it out somehow, I don't know how."

Jenny groaned and flung herself into one of the chairs. "Perfect, that's—yes, yes that's exactly what I need right now. Shit."

Jim lifted a white container. "Mu shu, anyone?"

Jenny glared up at him—then smirked. "Fuck off, Jim.

Gimme that."

"You want to get dressed first?"

"Oh, I guess. Thanks for picking this up."

He nodded.

Jenny rose and went back to the bedroom, leaving Jim alone in the kitchen with rapidly cooling Chinese chicken that somehow summed up how he felt about this life right then—lukewarm, a little greasy, and while better than nothing, not exactly a feast.

The thought made him smile grimly. He opened the box and dug in with a plastic fork, feeling vaguely fraudulent somehow for not using chopsticks.

Glass broke.

Jim looked up, mouth full of food. He waited for Jenny to shout for help, but no shout came.

"What was that?" Darla called from the living room, where she clearly meant to stay.

Jim stood and walked to the hall, frowning. "Don't know. Jenny?"

Jenny didn't answer.

From the bedroom, Jim thought he heard a thump. What the—

Oh, fuck! he thought, and ran.

He turned into the bedroom and saw the bathroom door was shut, but something thumped again inside. Adrenalin flooded his system as he tried the door. It was unlocked, but he could only open it a quarter-inch. Something heavy blocked its swing, and pushed it shut again.

It's him. It's Brother.

These words were not actual words in his head; they took the form of images and nonsense sounds that swirled around like blood in a drain.

"*Jenny!*"

Impulsively, he kicked the door as hard as he could just below the doorknob. Something grunted and the door opened partially. Jim caught a glance of something brown and rough-woven, some piece of clothing.

In the gap, he heard Jenny choking on a scream, calling for him through a gurgle. Swearing, his vision beginning to tunnel, Jim threw his entire weight against the bathroom door.

Jenny lay naked on the floor. Her towel bunched beneath her hips. She clawed at the tub, trying to pull herself up with one hand while massaging her throat with the other.

Beyond her, also on the ground, was a man.

SEVEN

The stranger wore mostly brown, or else whatever colors the clothes had once been had morphed to brown after years of not washing. He was the very picture of homelessness: a thick, wiry gray beard, skin tanned taut and red by the sun, clothes soiled with unknown fluids, teeth yellow and black. A sharp, rancid smell rose from him, assaulting Jim's senses under the lavender and flowery scents lingering from Jenny's shower.

"What the fuck!" Jim roared, but didn't move. The unreality of the moment clamped him in place. This kind of shit just didn't happen. Right? Right?

Might wanna ask Travis about that, his guts snickered at him.

So this was Brother.

The man grinned and snarled at the same time and launched himself at Jim. Still incapacitated by his brain's inability to respond, Jim stood there and let the attack hit him full force in the body. The man's crushing blow drove them to the bed, the man on top, hands wrapped around Jim's throat.

Jim heard Jenny screaming and the sounds of his own muffled gurgling, but nothing else. The man above him leered down, grinning. Even as his breath choked deep in his throat, Jim could see the man was well beyond sanity; the blue of his eyes shone brightly like an animal's, whose only impulses were feeding and fucking. Which of these he was about to do Jim, he couldn't tell.

Jim's body finally fought back without him, determined to preserve itself despite his fear. He pulled hard at the man's arms. He pried and bent and twisted, but the homeless man's strength was preternatural. Jim could feel that the man's arms were much thinner than his own, but his muscles were fueled by something far stronger. Hate, perhaps, or madness. It was the stringy strength of a man whose body was his primary tool for survival. He didn't have to fear a heart attack from too much sitting in an air conditioned office.

Jim couldn't fight him.

The man was too strong, too determined. Jim's vision corkscrewed as his mind sent frantic warnings: not enough air, shutdown imminent, red alert red alert—

Jim drove his right knee upward.

Whatever else the man might be, he was still a man. Jim felt his testicles smashing flat for a moment under the momentum of his knee.

The man barked and rolled away. Jim scooted back, bunching up the comforter beneath him, holding his throat. He took deep, scathing breaths that seemed cradled in fire.

Seeing the man in agony pleased him. Since his knees were still bent from scooting backward, Jim used the potential energy to fire a kick into his attacker's face. Either he was too weak from fear or the man was too focused on his balls, but the kick didn't do much. Still—it felt good to try.

Jim checked on Jenny. She was on her feet, but unsteady. Jenny hovered over the tub, half-bent, holding her breasts with her left forearm and steadying herself on the counter with her right hand.

"Cops," Jim coughed. "Call the . . . cops. Get—Darla—"

Jenny, her face strained tight, stumbled toward the bathroom door. She hesitated when she saw she'd have to pass the homeless man to get out of the room and to her cell, which was still in the kitchen.

Jim forced himself up and spun around wildly, looking for some way to tie up their assailant until the cops came.

Way to go, his brain cheered as he rushed to Jenny's bureau and pawed through it. *Way to go, Jimbo, you're the hero of this story! You see me there, Jen? You see what I did? Fuck yeah, I got this!*

"Mom!"

Jim whipped around. Jenny screamed Darla's name.

Darla stood in the threshold between Jenny's bedroom and the hallway. Her arms were straight down at her sides. Darla's eyes were wide and unblinking, her throat pulsing with fast gasps of breath. She sounded as if she were having an asthma attack.

Does Darla have asthma? Jim thought with animal stupidity. *That's—*

Then he understood.

Jim could only barely process what he was seeing: Clawed hands held Darla's upper arms flat against her sides. A crouched figure hunkered behind her, as if using her as a human shield. As he stared, Jim's hands went cold, then his feet, then the rest of his limbs as someone peeked up and over Darla's shoulder.

Its hair stuck up and waved like a baby's, fine and translucent. Its head seemed pointed at the crown, or else its slick, sloped forehead gave that impression. The eyes were blue, as brilliant as Travis's had been just days ago; as brilliant as Darla's were now.

But as it continued to lift its head higher, Jim realized this thing was only next-door to human, some cousin of humanity, not the real thing.

The skin around its mouth pulled backward tightly, like a face-lift gone terribly wrong. Its mouth was small, firm, and circular. Jim could make out tiny triangular teeth behind its thin lips. The thing moved its jaw up and down, but the mouth didn't seem able to close all the way; doing so would strain its skin to the point of tearing.

It may have been talking, but Jim couldn't tell over Jenny's screams and threats.

"Let her go! Let her go you fucker I'll kill you I swear to God you fucking let her go—!"

The homeless man rose and backhanded her. Jim crouched, ready to attack . . . but he stopped, shooting a glance back at the thing holding Darla.

Jenny stepped back, holding her face. The homeless man pointed at Jim while massaging his groin with his other hand.

"Don't," he said. "Just sit down, boy."

"Mommy?" Darla gasped.

The situation changed then. Jim felt it in the air before anything happened.

Jenny raised her hands toward her daughter. "Okay! Okay. Please. Please. Just don't hurt her. I'll give you anything you want just don't hurt my daughter."

Jim darted his eyes between them all. So too, it seemed, did the monster behind Darla.

No—not just a monster.

Brother.

This was Brother, not the crusty homeless motherfucker who'd attacked them. Maybe he was related too, somehow. Not that it mattered at the moment.

The homeless guy lifted a filthy eyebrow at Jenny, his gaze taking in her naked body. Jenny glared back at him, trembling.

The guy turned to Jim. "On the floor, boy."

Jim licked his lips and again took stock of the scene. Goddammit, he was not trained for this kind of scenario! He could try to rush Brother and Darla, knock them apart, give Darla a chance to run. No one had any weapons—well, except for the two-inch brown curved talons sticking out of Brother's fingers. They may have been fingernails, left to grow and mutate and snap off.

So his assets included himself—a lanky desk jockey—a naked woman, and a twelve-year-old girl being held still by a mutant.

"Okay," Jim said. He lifted his hands to show they were empty as he slowly knelt on the floor. "Okay, I'm going. Don't hurt them."

"Oh, shut the fuck up." The homeless man booted him in the face. Jim grunted and hit the ground.

The man knelt on his back forcing a cough out of Jim's lungs. "Hands behind your back," the man ordered. To Jenny, he snapped, "You, on the bed, face-down, don't move. You hear me?"

Jim twisted his head, nose brushing the carpet, and watched Jenny climbing onto the mattress. She didn't make a sound. From his vantage, he could now only see the soles of her feet.

The guy rummaged around in the drawers Jim had

opened. Something slithered past Jim's arm, and then one of Jenny's thin leather belts bound his wrists behind him. Grinding his knees into Jim's back, the man spun and did the same to Jim's ankles.

With a grunt, the man got up. He stood over Jim, hunched. "You really cracked my nuts, boy. God damn. Yeah, you did."

He fired another boot against Jim's cheek. Jim heard the crack of his cheekbone fracturing, his vision going dark. It felt like a brick had smashed his face.

When he was able to open his eyes again, Jim saw the man was crawling onto the mattress with three more belts and scarves dangling from his hand. Jim knew exactly what was next.

Oh, Christ, no, he thought. Jesus, Jesus, no.

"Please," he heard Jenny saying. She was not screaming, and not even begging. "Please let my daughter go now, I'll do anything you want."

"Yup," the man said. Jim saw him straddling her back. "I know you will, sugar."

"Let her go!" Jim shouted, pointlessly.

"Ah, shut your fuck hole," the man said, casting only the barest of glances behind him. "You fucked up my balls. I need 'em looked after."

"Jesus, man, then let the *kid* go!" Jim roared. He pulled hard against his restraints. The belt around his ankles seemed to slip a bit, but he wasn't sure. "Don't make her stand there!"

"That ain't up to me, that's up to my little buddy there."

Jim snaked his body to the left to better see Darla and Brother. They hadn't moved from the threshold. Darla glanced down at him, her face tight as she breathed noisily between her teeth. He tried to will her to fight, to struggle, but either Brother was too strong or she was too scared.

The man grunted. Jim turned toward the bed again, his heart turning to ice—but the man was still clothed. The grunt had come from him tightening the belts around Jenny's hands, lashing her to the wrought iron headboard.

"No!" Jenny cried. "Please just don't hurt my daughter!"

The guy astride her laughed. "Hurt her? He ain't gonna hurt *her*. He's here to take care of her, you stupid bitch."

Take care of her? Jim thought madly. Take care . . . ?

He heard Jenny's voice muffle a moment later, and Jim realized the man had stuffed something into her mouth as a gag.

Oh, God, this is really happening. And when it's over this guy is going to kill us all. Or, at least the two of us. Take care of Darla, that's what he said, really? Why—?

Jenny issued a cry through the gag. Jim's body tensed. "Get the fuck off her, you bastard! I'm gonna fucking kill you!"

"No you ain't." The man slid off Jenny, pausing only long enough to slap her ass a couple times with one crusty hand. The gesture enraged Jim.

He nudged Jim onto his back. Jim felt the belt around his ankle slip a little more.

"Now as I was saying," the man said, tugging his pants down to reveal a long, narrow penis, white as an icicle against the rest of his tanned hands and face. "You racked my balls and I need them to feel better, so open up, boy."

Jim blinked, struggling to comprehend. As the man stroked his dick over Jim, his intent crystalized.

Jim's mind sent up flares. Jenny was safe—safe-ish—for the moment, he wasn't going to rape her. Darla had not been physically harmed . . .

There was something he could do, there was something . . . something he'd missed.

Brother.

Brother was here to take care of Darla—to *care for* her. He wasn't going to hurt her. Under any circumstances? Well, that he couldn't know for sure. But in Brother's mind, he was helping her. He was being protective, not violent.

That meant Darla was not a chip on the table. The homeless guy was still a threat, but probably not to Darla, not directly.

He was somehow *working* for Brother.

Yes, yes, that's it, Jim chanted silently as the man's erection took shape in his leathery hand. Brother had assaulted the people who'd hurt him, who'd ignored him. Jenny was not on that list, just like Beard had said. Neither was Darla. No, Darla was a relative, a child, and Brother was going to protect her from any and every person in the family who could even theoretically hurt *her*.

How this motherfucker with the shit-stained clothes was involved, Jim didn't know and couldn't guess. And as the man began to bend over Jim's face, he figured, well, it probably wasn't important right now.

The belt came loose from his ankles.

Jim struck.

EIGHT

Using muscles he'd long forgotten existed, Jim curled his feet upward off the floor and slammed them into the man from behind. Caught off-guard and with his pants still puddled around his ankles, the man stumbled forward and crashed into the wall.

Jim tossed himself to the right and managed to get to a kneeling position. The man cursed and spun, his erection bobbing ridiculously before him. Jim launched himself, driving a shoulder into the man's midsection. They smashed into the wall together, groaning and growling like animals.

"Run!" Jim screamed, hoping Darla knew it was her he was instructing.

But he couldn't turn to look. The man snarled something foul and brought his fists thumping down across Jim's back, knocking more breath from his lungs again. Christ, this malnourished stringy bastard was fucking *winning*.

Years of passive ingestion of movies and television finally

served a purpose: he understood right then that this man was, in fact, a killer. Either he'd done it before, or wouldn't mind giving it a try. Whatever his connection to Brother, he must have known what Brother was doing this past week.

If you don't stop him right here, right now, he will absolutely kill you, Jim's brain calmly informed him. You know that.

So make sure he can't.

Jim lunged and bit.

The man's index finger came off surprisingly easy, though that was likely due to the adrenalin coursing through Jim's body. His teeth clamped down and masticated until meeting together again, a full inch of bone and flesh in his mouth.

He straightened and spit out the finger. The man mewed plaintively, kitten-like, as blood rocketed from the stump in a flood of crimson that splashed on the carpet. His free hand cupped beneath the wound but did not touch it, as if he were afraid of causing more damage.

Jim whipped around, savage, lips pulled back, searching for Darla.

She was gone.

So was Brother.

The man whimpered behind him and fell to his knees.

Breathing hard, Jim struggled against the belt wrapped around his arms. It came off with relative ease, and he shook his hands free. Twisting his right shoulder back, he swung the mightiest fist he could manage at the man's face.

The punch connected solidly. The blow sent the man's head twisting practically over his shoulder. With a soft grunt, he fell forward in the squishy pool of his own blood.

Jim raced to Jenny, wiping blood off his face with his forearm as he went, spitting again. He yanked one of her hands free.

"He's got Darla!" Jim shouted, and left Jenny to undo the rest of her binding. "Tie that fucker up!"

By then he was in the hall, running hard for the living room.

Nothing. The TV blared Darla's show, that was all.

He dodged into the kitchen. Nothing—but the garage door was open.

"Darla!" He kicked the door wider and threw himself inside.

There.

Brother had nowhere else to go. He'd backed into a corner with Darla still held out in front of him like a shield. Darla didn't look harmed, just terrified.

Jim instantly lifted his hands in a peaceful gesture, then quickly wiped blood from his chin again, trying to look less frightening—if anything indeed could frighten the monster he was looking at.

"Okay, okay," he said, trying to sound gentle but gasping each syllable. "We can work this out. All right? We can work something out."

Brother peered at him over Darla's shoulder. Jim could not read his expression at all, although his posture suggested he was at the very least a bit worried. Considering all he was capable off, Jim had to believe he was nominally feral, and that he'd act like a trapped animal if pushed any farther.

On the other hand, he'd also managed to break into three locations and mutilate people without being caught, so he was not devoid of intelligence.

Watch your step, Jim thought.

"What's your name?" No one had mentioned one.

Brother blinked and tilted his head.

Jesus, he doesn't have a name . . . or he doesn't even understand the question. What the hell did they do to you?

Jim kept his eyes on the pair in the corner while letting his periphery scan the rest of the garage. They didn't have much room to maneuver; his Jeep and Jenny's car took up most of the available space. Brother and Darla were backed into the furthest possible corner opposite the kitchen door. Landscaping tools hung from friction clamps on the wall behind them, and red plastic bins were stacked in a rack overhead. The garage door opener was mounted on the wall by the door, near Jim, and there were no windows. The only way out was back through the house.

Through me, Jim thought sickly. God, how do we end this well? How?

The gun.

His Glock was in the Jeep still, but locked up and unloaded. Under the best of circumstances, it would take him well over a minute to get into the car, unlock the case, slap a magazine in and rack it. Too long.

"Please do something," Darla whispered. Her voice shook.

Jim nodded and risked a slow step closer. Brother didn't react.

"You're worried about her, aren't you?" Jim asked. "That's why you came here. To take care of her?"

Brother nodded. Okay, good; he understood the fucking language, that was a start . . .

Brother let go of one of Darla's arms, but Jim saw his other hand squeeze harder. He wasn't letting her go. He raised the free hand, his left, to his eye and tapped one claw near his eyeball.

Christ, what does that mean? Jim raged silently. Then he switched gears: No, wait—Jenny will be on the phone with the cops any second now if she isn't already. They'll be here soon. Just got to keep Darla safe and Brother busy. Then they'll take it from there.

Brother wasn't waiting that long.

Darla came flying toward Jim, screeching. Jim pinwheeled backward as she crashed into him. They fell to the concrete in a tangle.

"Fuck!" Jim cried, trying to right himself. He got a handful of Darla's rugby shirt and hauled upward as best he could, aiming to get her toward the door. "Go!"

She managed to land a foot in his midsection as she pushed herself up. Jim grunted and doubled up, still on his ass.

Darla tumbled into the kitchen. "Come on!"

"Close the—!" Jim began, but then the breath coughed out of him as Brother tackled him flat.

He heard the door shut. Good girl.

Then came bright white terror as he realized he was pinned to the ground beneath Brother and his claws. Those claws that had torn out three pairs of eyes.

"Oh, fuck," Jim whined. "Fuck, no, please—"

He struggled against Brother's weight, but the mutation clearly knew what he was doing. Jim was more immobile now than when he'd been tied up with Jenny's belts.

Brother tilted his head again, bird-like. Jim could smell the warm breath bellowing out of his mouth-hole, a green and fetid cloud that made Jim want to vomit as he thought about the smell of eyeballs crushed in Brother's maw.

"I'm begging you," he grunted. "Don't do it, don't."

Brother tipped his head the other way, as if trying to comprehend.

He raised a hand. The claw shone dully under the garage light that had popped on when they entered.

Jim squeezed his eyes shut—then opened them wide instead. No need to blind himself before the moment arrived . . .

Staring down at him, Brother pricked the corner of his own eye. A drop of blood appeared, then grew to a flow as Brother pushed harder.

Jim's mouth fell open in shock. Blood ran down Brother's arm and dripped from his elbow, landing on Jim's face. Jim shut his mouth in response.

Then Brother dug in.

Jim turned away, but it did little good. Brother shrieked in agony as he dug the claw into his own eye socket and worked his finger like key in a lock.

"God, fuck, ugh!" Jim groaned as more blood and thick fluid poured down Brother's arm, coating Jim's face. Drops landed in his ear, partially deafening him.

Jim wrestled himself back and forth, praying for some room to knock this creature off of him. Only distantly did it occur to him that this was, at least, better than his own eyes being ripped out.

He thought her heard a pop as Brother pulled the eye out and dangled it in front of Jim. Brother was panting now, fast agonized breaths, and Jim could hardly believe he'd managed the operation while remaining conscious.

Brother gripped Jim's mouth. His head become frozen in place. Great Christ, his *strength* . . .

It took only a second for Brother to wrench Jim's mouth open. Jim fought uselessly against him.

Brother gazed at him with his one eye, pitying somehow . . . then forced his half-mashed eyeball into Jim's mouth.

Jim screamed as best was possible as Brother switched his grip to clamp Jim's mouth shut.

My God what hell is this, what hell is this, Jim's mind chanted at him as hot puke worked its way up his throat. No, no, don't puke, you'll choke, oh fuck, don't puke—

Contracting every muscle in his body, Jim swallowed. The organ was warm and slick, salty somehow, perhaps with tears or blood or both. Pretend it's an oyster, pretend it's anything, oh *God!*

He went deaf.

He went deaf and entered some fourth dimension, some netherworld where everything in sight was inverted. He could breathe easily again, so that was nice. The weight was gone from his body.

Jim rolled over and pulled himself lupine, looking at the kitchen door.

A uniformed cop stood in the doorway, weapon raised. Smoke drifted from the barrel as the cop stared past Jim.

Jim turned to look.

Brother lay on his back, motionless, his head twisted to one side, the side facing Jim. In addition to the cavernous black hole of his empty eye socket, another hole had opened up in his chest, only mildly bloody, but Brother's chest didn't move. Brother was dead.

Jim turned away, stared blankly at the concrete floor, and vomited until he ruptured a blood vessel in his eye.

NINE

Jim stood up from the café table when Beard entered. The men shook hands.

"Get you anything?" Jim asked.

"No no, I'm fine. Thanks."

They sat.

"Thank you for meeting me here," Jim said.

"I knew you'd want to know."

"Did you tell Jenny and Travis?"

Beard sat back. "I did. You've not spoken to them?"

"Not really. Jenny and I are over. Which is fine. For the best. I don't think either of us could really have a relationship any time soon after all this. So the homeless guy . . ."

"Burt Standford. Been on the streets for thirty, thirty-five years. Living underground."

"That sounded literal."

"Yes. Literally. There's a lot more underground space in Phoenix than you might think. We don't broadcast it."

Jim blew out a sigh. He didn't want to know, really. "Why was he helping Travis's brother?"

"Still piecing that together. They had a relationship of some kind, from a long time ago. At the moment, it looks like Standford found the boy when the Montroses got rid of him. Took him in, raised him up. If you could call it that. I can't imagine just how mentally damaged the kid was after what his parents did, then you add in homelessness on top of it, being coached on survival by a guy like Standford . . ."

Beard shook his head.

"But Standford, he'll be in jail?"

"The rest of his life, whatever's left of it. Might be better off there, really. He didn't contest anything, but he's also not entirely sane, so, we'll see where that goes. But yeah. You don't have to worry about him again."

Beard cleared his throat and leaned forward.

"Listen, not for nothing, but you might want to get some help after all this. You know? Professional help. Even if you don't think you need it."

"Oh, I need it." Jim half-grinned. "Don't worry, I am. Didn't eat anything for a week, but."

Beard offered him a sympathetic dry chuckle.

"Why'd he do that?" Jim asked suddenly. "It's the piece I can't figure out. Why would the brother make me . . . ?"

Beard shook his head again. "No way to know, I'm afraid. But my feeling is he was done. He was cornered, and he knew it. I think maybe he was either making amends or . . . or just doing what he thought the entire Montrose family deserved, which included him. Who knows. Sorry I can't answer that."

Jim nodded. "Well, thanks for coming."

Beard stood. "No problem. We shouldn't need anything else from you. I hope everything works out."

"Thank you."

Beard tipped him a nod and walked out of the café. Jim watched him through the windows and let him drive out of the lot before leaving himself.

He still had to hit the library to pick up some more audiobooks for Travis.

Tom Leveen is a Bram Stoker Award finalist and an award-winning novelist. He has also written for the comic book series *Spawn*. For free books and more information, visit:

linktr.ee/tomleveen

If you enjoyed this book, please consider leaving a review. Thank you very much!

www.ingramcontent.com/pod-product-compliance
Lightning Source LLC
Chambersburg PA
CBHW030355180626
46812CB00007B/2890